D1242366

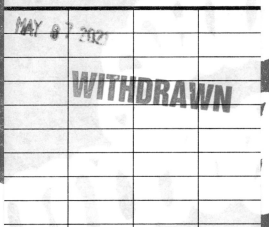

TELEPHONE
tales

GIANNI RODARI
TELEPHONE
tales

ILLUSTRATED BY
VALERIO VIDALI

TRANSLATED FROM THE ITALIAN BY
ANTONY SHUGAAR

Enchanted Lion Books
NEW YORK

Once upon a time there was …

… a man named Signor Bianchi from Varese. He was an accountant who worked as a traveling salesman, and six days out of every seven, he crisscrossed all of Italy—east, west, south, north, and central—selling pharmaceuticals. Every Sunday, he returned home, and Monday morning, he set out again on his rounds. But before he left, his daughter always told him,

"Remember, Papa, a story every night before bed."

That little girl couldn't sleep without a bedtime story, and her mama had already told her all the stories she knew, most of them three times already. And so, every evening—no matter where he was—at nine o'clock on the dot, Signor Bianchi put in a phone call to Varese and told his little girl a story. This book, in fact, contains all of Signor Bianchi's stories. You may notice that they're all rather short. There's a reason for that: Signor Bianchi was an accountant, and he was paying for all those phone calls out of his own pocket, so he couldn't afford to make extended long-distance phone calls. Only occasionally, if he'd wrapped up some very good sales, could he afford a few extra long-distance "clicks."

I'm told that when Signor Bianchi called Varese, all the young ladies who worked the telephone switchboard simply stopped putting calls through, so they could listen to his stories. I bet they did—some of them are really not half bad.

THE UNLUCKY HUNTER

"Get your rifle, Giuseppe. Get your rifle and go hunting," a woman told her young son one fine morning. "Your sister is getting married tomorrow, and she wants to dine on rabbit and polenta."

Giuseppe got his rifle and went hunting. The first thing he saw was a rabbit hopping out from under a hedge and bounding into a field. He pointed his rifle, took careful aim, and pulled the trigger. But the rifle said, "Boom!"—just like that, with a human voice. And instead of firing the bullet out of the barrel, it simply let it tumble to the ground.

Giuseppe picked up the bullet and stared at it in amazement. Then he closely examined the rifle, and really, it looked as it usually did. All the same, instead of firing, it had just exclaimed, "Boom!" in a cheerful, fresh little voice. Giuseppe peered down the barrel. *How could this be? Come on now! Could someone be hiding in that gun? No, sure enough, there was no one down that barrel—no one and nothing.*

"But my mama wants a rabbit. And my sister wants to eat it with polenta ..."

Just then, the same rabbit as before strolled by, right in front of Giuseppe, only this time it had a white veil over its head dotted with orange blossoms, and it kept its eyes down as it minced along, taking tiny, little steps.

"Well, what do you know," said Giuseppe. "The rabbit is getting married too. Oh well, I guess I'll just go shoot a pheasant."

He went a little farther along through the woods and,

indeed, happened upon a pheasant promenading down the trail unafraid, like on the first day of hunting season, before the pheasants even know what a rifle is.

Giuseppe took aim, pulled the trigger, and the rifle went, "Bam!" It said, "Bam! Bam!" twice, just like a little boy would have done with his wooden rifle. The bullet fell to the ground and scared a few red ants, who immediately scurried to hide under a pine tree.

"Oh well, isn't this fine," said Giuseppe as he started to lose his temper. "My mama will certainly be well-pleased if I come home with an empty game bag."

The pheasant—who at the sound of that "Bam! Bam!" had raced into the underbrush—reappeared on the trail, and this time, he was followed by his little ones parading in single file, all of them in the mood to laugh. Behind them all strutted their mother, proud and pleased as if she'd just been awarded first prize for her brood.

"Oh sure, I'll bet you're happy with the way things are going," grumbled Giuseppe. "You've been married for a while now. But what am I supposed to shoot at?"

He painstakingly reloaded his rifle and looked in all directions. There was nothing but a blackbird on a branch, whistling as if to say, "Shoot me! Shoot me!"

So, Giuseppe shot. But the rifle said, "Bang!" like a little kid reading a comic book. And it added a small noise you would have sworn was a giggle. The blackbird whistled even more cheerfully than before, as if to say, "You fired your gun, you heard the sound, the bullet is lying on the ground."

"Just as I expected," said Giuseppe. "Evidently, the rifles have all gone on strike today."

"How did your hunting go, Giuseppe?" his mother asked him when he returned home.

"Oh fine, Mama. I landed three big, fat disappointments. I'm sure they'll be delicious with a bowl of polenta."

THE
ICE CREAM
PALACE

Once upon a time in Bologna, they built an ice cream palace right on the main square: the Piazza Maggiore. The roof was made of whipped cream, the smoke rising from the chimney tops was made of spun sugar, and the chimneys themselves were made of candied fruit. All the rest was ice cream: ice cream doors, ice cream walls, ice cream furniture. Children came from near and far to have a lick of ice cream.

One tiny child latched onto a table and licked the table legs one by one, until the table collapsed on top of him with all the dishes, and the dishes were made of chocolate ice cream, the most delicious kind.

A policeman working in City Hall eventually noticed that a window was melting. The window panes were made of strawberry ice cream, and it was streaming down in pink rivulets.

"Hurry!" cried the policeman. "Hurry, scurry, twice as fast!"

And everyone rushed over to lick as fast as they could to keep even a single drop of that masterpiece from going to waste.

"A chair!" pleaded a little old lady who couldn't fight her way through the mob. "A chair for a poor old woman. Who'll bring me a chair? An armchair with armrests, if possible."

A generous fireman hurried to get her a vanilla-and-pistachio ice cream armchair, and the poor little old lady contentedly started licking away at it, starting right from the armrests.

That was a magnificent day for one and all, and by doctor's orders, no one had a tummy ache.

Even now, when children ask for another ice cream, their parents sigh, "Okay, okay, but to keep you satisfied, we would need a whole palace made of ice cream, just like the one in Bologna!"

A DISTRACTIBLE CHILD GOES FOR A WALK

"Mama, I'm going out for a walk."

"Go right ahead, Giovanni, but look both ways when you cross the street."

"All right, Mama. Bye-bye, Mama."

"You're always so distractible."

"Yes, Mama. Bye-bye, Mama."

Giovanni goes cheerfully out the door, and for the first block or so, he pays close attention, stopping every so often to check he hasn't lost anything.

"Am I all here? Yes, I am!" and he laughs happily to himself.

He's so pleased with how careful he's being that he starts hopping along like a sparrow. Soon enough, though, he's completely captivated, staring at shop windows, cars, the clouds—and naturally, trouble follows.

A gentleman very politely scolds him, "Oh, young man, you're so distractible. You see? You've already lost a hand."

"Yes, sir, you're right. I'm so distractible."

He starts searching for his hand, but instead, he finds an empty tin can. Is the can really empty? Let's take a look. What could have been in it before it was empty? It can't possibly have been empty right from the very first day …

Giovanni forgets about looking for his hand, and then he forgets about the tin can, too, because he's spotted a dog with a limp, and in his hurry to catch up with the limping dog before it turns the corner, he loses a whole arm. But he doesn't even notice and just keeps running.

12

A nice woman calls after him, "Giovanni, Giovanni, your arm!"

But, of course, he pays her no mind.

"Oh, well," says the nice woman. "I'll take it to his mama." And she goes to Giovanni's mama's house.

"Signora, I've brought you your son's arm."

"Oh, he's so distractible. I just don't know what to say or do anymore."

"Well, it's no mystery. That's just the way children are."

A little while later, another nice woman comes over to visit. "Signora, I found a foot. It wouldn't belong to your boy, Giovanni, would it?"

"Why, of course it's his. I recognize it from that shoe with a hole in the sole. Oh, what a distractible child God gave me. I just don't know what to say or do anymore."

"Well, it's no mystery. That's just the way children are."

Then a little old lady comes by, and the baker's delivery boy, and a trolley conductor, and even a retired schoolteacher, and they all bring some piece or other of Giovanni: a leg, an ear, a nose.

"Has there ever been a boy as distractible as my son Giovanni?"

"Well, Signora, that's just the way children are."

At last, Giovanni himself comes in, hopping on just one leg, with no ears or arms, but as cheerful as a sparrow, as he always is, and his mother shakes her head, puts him back together, and gives him a kiss.

"Is anything missing, Mama? Have I been a good boy?"

"Yes, Giovanni, you've been a very good boy."

13

A BUILDING
FOR BREAKING

Once upon a time in Busto Arsizio, the people were worried because the children were breaking everything. Let's not even mention how they routinely wore out the soles of their shoes, the knees of their trousers, or their school book bags. But now they were breaking windows when playing ball, plates at the dinner table, and glasses at the café. The only reason they didn't break the walls of the houses was that they didn't have sledgehammers with which to do it.

The parents had no idea what to do or say anymore, so they turned to the mayor.

"Shall we write them tickets?" suggested the mayor.

"Yes, let's. What a great idea," said the parents, who were at their wit's end. "Then we can use the broken windows and plates to pay those tickets."

Luckily, there are plenty of accountants around Busto Arsizio. In fact, there's an accountant for every three people, and the accountants are all very good at accounting for things. But the accountant who was better at accounting than any of his colleagues was Signor Gamberoni, an elderly gentleman with plenty of grandchildren and, therefore, extensive experience when it came to broken windows and broken plates. He took a sheet of paper and a pencil and reckoned up all the damages that the children of Busto Arsizio had caused by shattering and breaking so many fine and useful objects. The sum he came up with was truly frightening: eleventy thousand sporty-seven hundred and thirty-three.

"With half this money," Signor Gamberoni, the accountant,

14

explained, "we can construct a building just for breaking and order the children to knock it to bits. If this approach doesn't cure them, nothing ever will."

The proposal was accepted, and the building was constructed lickety-split, as sure as two plus two equals four. It stood seven stories tall, it had ninety-nine rooms, and every room was filled to the rafters with cabinets and dressers that were packed solid with utensils and bric-a-brac, to say nothing of the mirrors and faucets throughout the house. On the day the building was inaugurated, every child in Busto Arsizio was given a sledgehammer. At a signal from the mayor, the doors to the building for breaking were thrown wide open.

It's too bad that television news crews didn't get there in time to broadcast what followed. The people who saw it with their own eyes and heard it with their own ears assure us that it seemed like the outbreak of the Third World War—may such a thing never happen! The children rampaged from room to room like the army of Attila the Hun, swinging their sledgehammers and smashing to smithereens anything that came within reach. You could hear the noise all over Lombardy and through half of Switzerland. Children no taller than a cat's tail started banging away at cupboards the size of a battleship and demolished them with such thoroughness that there was nothing left but a pile of sawdust. Children from the local nursery school, lovely and rosy-cheeked in their pink and blue smocks, diligently smashed expensive china coffee sets, pulverizing the demitasse cups and saucers into a fine dust that they then used to powder their noses.

At the end of the first day, not a single glass or cup remained intact. At the end of the second day, they were starting to run out of chairs. At the end of the third day, the children set to work on the walls, starting with the top floor, but by the time they'd worked their way down to the fifth floor—dead-tired and covered with dust like Napoleon's soldiers in the Egyptian desert—they dropped what they were doing and staggered home, trooping off to bed without stopping for dinner. By this point, they'd truly vented every destructive impulse, and the fun had completely gone out of breaking things. They'd suddenly become as delicate and light as butterflies. Had they played a soccer game on a field of crystal glasses, they wouldn't have chipped a single one.

Signor Gamberoni, the accountant, reckoned up the damages and proved that the city of Busto Arsizio had saved a grand total of two mega million and seven-and-a-half inches.

The city government allowed the citizens to do whatever they wished with what was left of the building. And so you would see certain distinguished gentlemen with leather briefcases and bifocal eyeglasses—judges, lawyers, managing directors—grab a sledgehammer and hurry in to demolish a wall or dismantle a staircase, smashing with such gusto that with every blow of the hammer, they felt years younger.

"Instead of fighting with your wife!" they said cheerfully.

"Instead of breaking ashtrays or the set of good china, which was a gift from Aunt Mirina ..." —followed by tremendous whacks of the sledgehammer.

The city of Busto Arsizio, as a sign of its gratitude, ordered a silver medal with a hole in the center issued to Signor Gamberoni, the accountant.

THE LITTLE OLD LADY
WHO COUNTED SNEEZES

Once upon a time in Gavirate, there was a little old lady who spent her days counting other people's sneezes. After, she'd tell her girlfriends the results of her calculations, and then they'd sit for hours and gossip about them.

"The pharmacist sneezed seven times in a row," the little old lady told her friends.

"I don't believe it!"

"I swear it's true, may my nose fall off my face if I'm telling a lie. He did it at five minutes to noon."

So, they'd talk and talk and talk, and when they were done, they all agreed that the pharmacist was watering down the cod liver oil he sold.

"The parish priest sneezed fourteen times in a row," the little old lady told them, her face red with excitement.

"You don't think you might have miscounted?"

"May my nose fall off my face if I missed a single sneeze."

"My, my, what's the world coming to!"

So, they'd talk and talk and talk, and when they were done, they all agreed that the parish priest put too much oil on his salad.

One time, the little old lady and all her girlfriends—there were more than seven of them—gathered and waited under the windows of Signor Delio, eager to eavesdrop. But Signor Delio never sneezed, not even once, because he didn't take snuff and he didn't have a cold.

"Not a single sneeze," said little old lady. "Something fishy is going on."

"Certainly," chorused her girlfriends.

But Signor Delio overheard them, and he took a great big handful of black pepper and dumped it into an old tin fly sprayer. Then, taking care not to be seen, he showered those old gossips where they were hiding, right outside his windowsill.

"Achoo!" went the little old lady.

"Achoo! Achoo!" went her girlfriends. And then they all dissolved into a chorus of sneezes, one after the other.

"I sneezed the most sneezes," said the little old lady.

"No, we sneezed more sneezes than you," retorted her girlfriend.

Yanking each other's hair, they hauled off and beat each other blue and green and yellow, tore each other's dresses, and lost a tooth each.

After that, the little old lady never spoke another word to her girlfriends. She bought a notebook and a pencil and went around the town all by herself, and for every sneeze she heard, she marked down an X.

When she died, they found that notebook full of X's, and they said, "Look at this. She must have marked down all her good deeds. Why, how many she did! If she doesn't go to Heaven, then nobody else will."

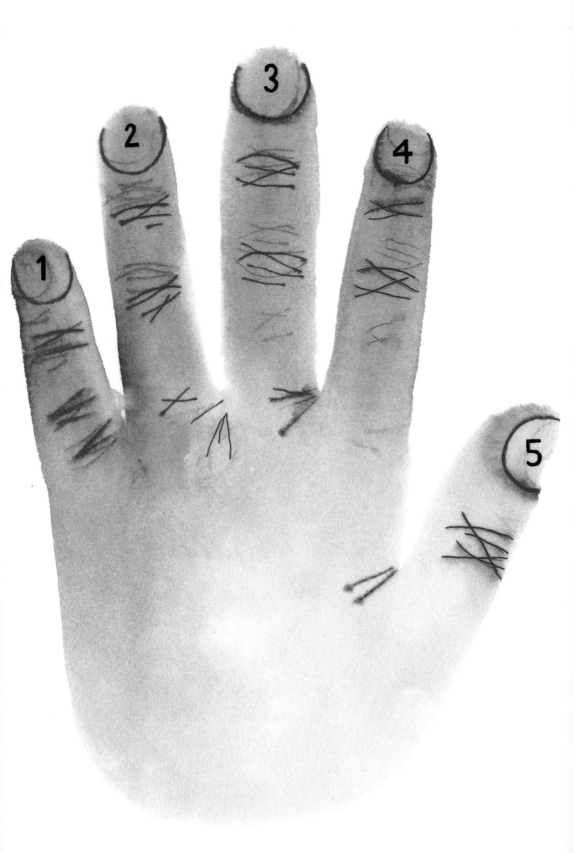

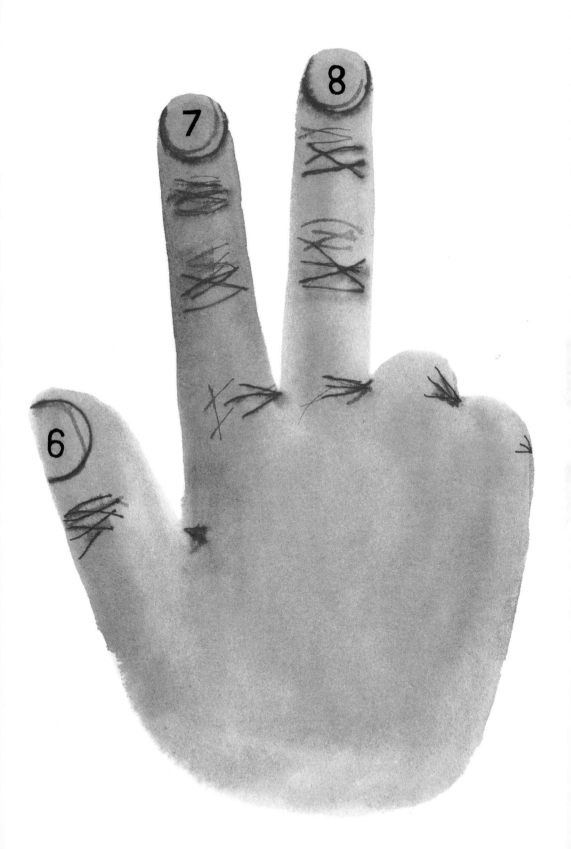

THE COUNTRY WITHOUT SHARP EDGES

Giovannino Vagabond was a great traveler. One day, in the course of his travels, he chanced upon a country where the corners of the houses were round and the roofs didn't rise to a point, but made a smooth, gentle hump instead. Rose bushes grew along the side of the road, and all at once, Giovannino decided he'd pick a rose and put it in his buttonhole. As he was picking the rose, he took great care not to prick his finger with the thorns, but he immediately noticed that the thorns didn't prick at all. There was no sharp point at the tip; in fact, the thorns seemed to be made of rubber, and they tickled his hand.

"Well, what do you think of that!" Giovannino exclaimed loudly.

Out from behind the rose bush popped a city constable, with a broad smile on his face. "Don't you know that it's forbidden to pick the roses?"

"I'm sorry. I just wasn't thinking."

"Then you'll only have to pay half a fine," said the constable, and with such a smile, he could have easily been the Little Butter Man who takes Pinocchio to Pleasure Island.

Giovannino noticed that the constable was writing out his ticket with a pencil that had no point, and he couldn't help but say: "Excuse me, but could I take a look at your saber?"

"Why, of course," said the constable. And of course, there was no sharp tip on the saber either.

"What country have I come to?" asked Giovannino.

"The Country without Sharp Edges," the constable replied

with such immense courtesy that all his words ought to have been written in capital letters.

"So, what do you do about nails?"

"Oh, we abolished them a long time ago. We do everything with glue. But now, if you please, slap me twice in the face."

Giovannino's jaw dropped, as if he were about to swallow a whole layer cake. "What? How can you say such a thing? I don't want to wind up behind bars for assaulting a constable. If anything, it's me who should be getting slapped in the face, not the other way around."

"No, this is how we do things here," the constable explained politely. "For a whole fine, four face slaps; for a half fine, just two."

"In the constable's face?"

"That's right, in the constable's face."

"But that's unfair. It's terrible."

"Certainly, it's unfair. Certainly, it's terrible," the constable replied. "It's such a despicable thing that people here are very careful not to break the law, because they would never want to slap a poor soul who's done nothing wrong. Come on now, give me those two slaps in the face, and next time, try to be more careful."

"But I don't even want to give you a pat on the cheek. If anything, I'd gently stroke your hair."

"In that case," the constable was forced to conclude, "I'll have to accompany you to the border."

And to Giovannino's great humiliation, he was forced to leave the Country without Sharp Edges. But to this very day, he still dreams of going back to a place where people live in such great courtesy and kindness, in lovely houses with gently rounded roofs.

23

THE COUNTRY
WITH AN
Un
IN FRONT

Giovannino Vagabond, the great traveler, traveled and traveled. One day, he chanced upon a country with an un in front.

"What kind of a country is this?" he asked one of its denizens, who was lazing in the shade of a tree.

The citizen replied by pulling a pencil sharpener out of his pocket, which he showed to Giovannino in the palm of his hand. "Do you see this?"

"It's a pencil sharpener."

"Completely wrong. It's actually a pencil unsharpener—that is, a pencil sharpener with an un in front. We use these to make pencils longer when they're worn down to a stub. They're very useful in schools, of course."

"Magnificent," said Giovannino. "What else do you have here?"

"We have clothes unhangers."

"You must mean something like a clothes hanger."

"Well, clothes hangers aren't particularly useful if you don't have a coat to hang on them. With our unhangers, everything's different. You don't have to hang anything on them, because there's already something hanging. If you need a coat, you just go and take it off. If someone needs a jacket, they don't even have to go buy one—they just go to the unhanger and unhang it. There are clothes unhangers for summer and clothes unhangers for winter; clothes unhangers for men and clothes unhangers for women. We save lots of money that way."

"How wonderful! What else?"

26

"Then we have the uncamera, which, instead of taking pictures, does caricatures, so you can laugh. And of course, we have the uncannon."

"Brrrr, that's scary."

"Not at all. The uncannon is just the opposite of a cannon, and it's good for unwaging war."

"How does it work?"

"It's super simple—even a child could use it. If there's a war, we blow the unbugle, we fire the uncannon, and the war is immediately unwaged."

What a wonderful place, the country with an un in front.

THE BUTTER MEN

Giovannino Vagabond, the great traveler and famous explorer, once chanced to visit the land of the butter men. If the butter men ventured out into the sunshine, they melted, so they always had to stay cool. In fact, they lived in a city where, instead of houses, there were lots of refrigerators. As Giovannino walked through the streets, he could see the butter men looking out from the portholes of their refrigerators with ice bags on their heads. On the door of each refrigerator was an intercom through which to speak.

"Hello?"

"Hello."

"Who is this?"

"I'm the king of the butter men. All Grade A cream. Milk from Swiss cows. Have you looked carefully at my refrigerator?"

"My word, it's solid gold. But don't you ever leave it and go outside?"

"In the winter, if it's cold enough, I go out in a car made of ice."

"But what if the sun happens to peek out suddenly from behind the clouds while Your Majesty is out for a ride?"

"It can't—it doesn't have permission. I'd order my soldiers to throw it in prison."

"Golly," said Giovannino. And he left that land and went to another.

ALICE TUMBLEDOWN

This is the story of Alice Tumbledown, who always tumbled everywhere.

Her grandfather was looking for her so he could take her to the park. "Alice! Where are you, Alice?"

"I'm right here, Grandpa."

" 'Here,' where?"

"Inside the alarm clock."

That's right. She'd opened the back hatch of the alarm clock to look around a little, and she'd wound up among the gears and springs. Now she was being forced to leap continuously from one place to another to keep from being crushed by all those mechanisms that clicked and clacked, going tick tock.

Another time, her grandfather was looking for her to give her an afternoon snack. "Alice! Where are you, Alice?"

"I'm right here, Grandpa."

" 'Here,' where?"

"Right here, inside the bottle. I was thirsty and fell in."

And in fact, there she was, swimming desperately to stay afloat. It's a good thing that the previous summer, at the beach of Sperlonga, she had learned to do the breaststroke.

"Hold on. I'll fish you out."

Her grandfather lowered a length of twine into the bottle. Alice grabbed on and clambered up it with great agility. She was someone who always got good grades in physical education.

On another occasion, Alice had actually disappeared. Her

grandfather was looking for her, her grandmother was looking for her, and even a neighbor woman, who always came over to read her grandfather's newspaper just to save a few coins, was looking for her.

"We'll be in big trouble if we don't find her before her parents come home from work," her grandmother murmured in fright.

"Alice! Alice! Where are you, Alice?"

But this time there was no answer, because Alice couldn't answer.

While poking around in the kitchen, she had fallen into the drawer where the silverware and napkins were kept, and she'd fallen asleep in there. Someone had shut the drawer without noticing her. When she woke up again, Alice found herself in the dark, but she wasn't afraid. After all, she'd once fallen down a drain, and it had been really dark in there.

Well, they're going to have to set the table for dinner, Alice thought. *And then they'll have to open the drawer.*

But nobody was thinking about dinner at all, precisely because Alice was missing. Her parents had come home from work, and they were berating her grandparents. "So this is how you babysit our daughter!"

"Our children never fell down the drains," the grandparents defended themselves. "Back in our day, they only fell out of bed and got a bump or two on the head."

Eventually, Alice got tired of waiting. She dug through the silverware, found the bottom of the drawer, and started stamping her foot. *Thump, thump, thump.*

"Hush, everyone, hush," said her father. "I hear thumping coming from somewhere."

Thump, thump, thump, Alice stamped.

What kisses, what hugs once they were reunited! As for Alice, she immediately took advantage of the opportunity to tumble into her father's jacket pocket, and by the time they got her back out, she'd gotten her face all smeared with ink by playing with his ballpoint pen.

THE ROAD OF CHOCOLATE

Once upon a time, three little brothers from Barletta were walking through the countryside when they found a road that was smooth as silk and dark brown from one end to the other.

"What could it be?" asked the first brother.

"It isn't wood," said the second brother.

"It isn't coal," said the third brother.

To get a better idea of what it was, they all three kneeled down and gave it a little lick.

Chocolate! A real road made out of chocolate. They started by eating a little piece, then another little piece, and by the time evening fell, the three brothers were still there, eating up the road, until there wasn't so much as a single square left, or even the smallest scrap of chocolate or road.

"Where are we?" asked the first brother.

"We aren't in Bari," said the second brother.

"We aren't in Molfetta," said the third brother.

They didn't know what to do. Luckily, they saw a farmer coming along on his cart.

"I'll take you home," said the farmer. And he took them all the way to Barletta, where he dropped them off right at their front door.

As they were getting out of the cart, they realized that the whole cart was made of gingerbread. Without stopping to say, "One, two," they began gobbling it up and didn't leave a single crumb—not even a wheel or an axle.

Never before in the town of Barletta had there been three such lucky little brothers, and who knows if there will ever be again?

INVENTING NUMBERS

"Shall we invent some numbers?"

"Yes, let's. I'll go first. Almost-one, almost-two, almost-three, almost-four, almost-five, almost-six."

"That's not enough. Listen to this one: a mega million times a billion, a tricyclon of squintillions, a googleplexity of centillions, and an octillion."

"All right, then, I'll invent a multiplication table: three times one, a barrel of fun; three times two, Kalamazoo; three times three, coffee and tea; three times four, dinosaur; three times five, backward dive; three times six, stacks of bricks; three times seven, manna from heaven; three times eight, Alexander the Great; three times nine, Frankenstein; three times ten, and back again."

"How much does this pasta cost?"

"Two slaps on the wrist."

"How far is it from here to Milan?"

"A thousand new miles, one used mile, and seven lemon gumdrops."

"How much does a teardrop weigh?"

"Depends. A willful child's teardrop weighs less than the wind, but that of a starving child weighs more than the world."

"How long is this story?"

"Too long."

"Okay, then, let's hurry up and invent more numbers. Here we go, in New York style: foist, secant, and toid, toity-toid and a hunnit and toid, a doity boid plus a noid is the woid."

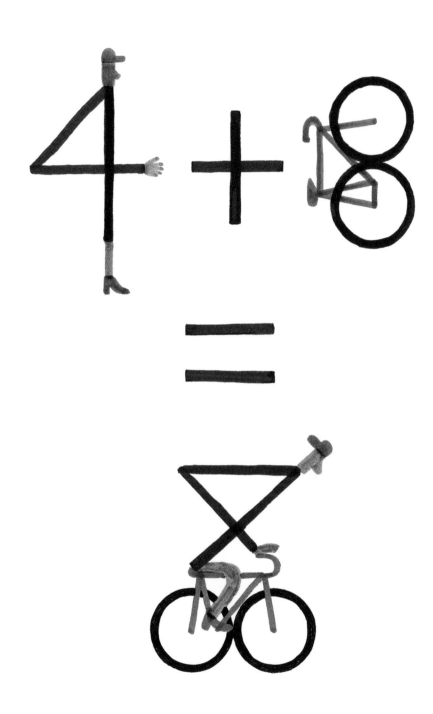

BRIF, BRAF, BRUF

Two little children in the quiet of the courtyard were playing at inventing a special new language that they could use to talk to each other so no one else would understand.

"Brif, braf," said the first child.

"Braf, brof," answered the second child. And they both burst out laughing.

On a second-story balcony was a kind old man reading his newspaper and looking out the window. Across the way was an old lady who was neither very kind nor very mean. "How silly these children are," said the lady.

But the kind old man disagreed. "I don't think they're silly."

"You're not going to tell me that you understood what they were saying?"

"I understood every word. The first child said, 'What a nice day.' And the second child replied, 'Tomorrow will be even nicer.'"

The old lady wrinkled her nose but said nothing, because the children had started talking again in their special language.

"Maraski, barabaski, pippirimoski," said the first child.

"Bruf," replied the second child. And they both burst out laughing again.

"You're not going to tell me that you understood this time, too!" exclaimed the old lady indignantly.

"I sure did—every word," answered the kind old man with a smile. "The first child said, 'How happy we are to be here on Earth.' And the second one answered, 'The world is beautiful.' "

"Is it really so beautiful?" insisted the old lady.

"Brif, braf, bruf," answered the kind old man.

BUYING THE CITY
OF STOCKHOLM

At the market of Gavirate, you will run into certain little men who see everything and understand everything, and there is no place on Earth where you'll find anyone who's better at selling things than they are.

One Friday afternoon, a little man came along who was selling all kinds of strange things: Mount Everest, the Indian Ocean, the seas of the moon. The little man had a wonderful spiel, and he was very persuasive, so before an hour had passed, he had nothing left to sell but the city of Stockholm.

He sold that to a barber in exchange for a shampoo and a haircut.

The barber hung up his certificate of ownership between two mirrors. It read: "Proud Owner of the City of Stockholm." Over time, the barber would eagerly point it out to his customers, answering all of their questions.

"It's a city in Sweden—the capital, in fact."

"Nearly a million people live there, and of course, they all belong to me."

"It looks out over the sea, but I'm not sure who owns that."

The barber saved up his pennies little by little, and last year, he finally went to Sweden to take a look at his property. The city of Stockholm looked wonderful to him, and the Swedes were very polite and kind. They couldn't understand a word of what he said, and he couldn't understand even half a word of what they said back to him.

"I am the owner of this city. Do you understand that or not? Didn't they send you the announcement?"

The Swedes all smiled back at him and nodded their heads. They couldn't understand him, but they had good manners. The barber rubbed his hands together and sighed with satisfaction. "What a beautiful city, and I traded just a shampoo and a haircut for it! I certainly got a bargain!"

But he was wrong: He had paid far too much for it. Because the whole world already belongs to every child that comes into it, and none had to pay even a penny for it. They need only to roll up their sleeves, stretch out their hands, and take it for themselves.

TOUCHING THE
KING'S NOSE

Once upon a time, Giovannino Vagabond decided to travel to
Rome to touch the king's nose. His friends urged him not to,
saying, "Listen to us. It's a dangerous thing to do. If the king
gets mad at you, you'll lose your nose, along with your whole
head."

But Giovannino had his mind made up. As he was pre-
paring his things to leave, to get in a little practice, he went
to see the local priest, the mayor, and the police commander,
and he touched each of their noses with such dexterity and
skill that none of them even noticed.

There you go. It's not really all that hard at all, thought
Giovannino.

When he arrived in the neighboring city, he asked the way
to the governor's house, the commissioner's house, and the
chief judge's house, and he went to pay a call on all three of
those illustrious personages. He touched each of their noses
with a finger or two as well. Those prominent citizens were a
little upset, because Giovannino seemed like such a well-be-
haved person and was comfortable talking about nearly any
topic you cared to name. The commissioner even got a bit
angry and exclaimed, "Are you trying to put my nose out of
joint?!"

"I'd never dream of such a thing," said Giovannino. "There
was a fly on it."

The commissioner looked around and saw neither flies nor
mosquitoes, but in the meantime, Giovannino made a hasty
bow and edged out the door, carefully shutting it behind him.

Giovannino had a notebook where he kept a record of the noses that he'd managed to touch—all of them prominent noses. But in Rome, the nose count rose so rapidly that Giovannino had to buy a bigger notebook. All he needed to do was walk down the street, and from here to there, he was certain to run into a couple of excellencies, several undersecretaries, and a dozen or so chiefs of staff.

To say nothing of commissioners: There were more commissioners than beggars, and all of those high-toned noses were well within reach. Moreover, their owners mistook Giovannino Vagabond's fleeting touch for a sign of respect for their authority, and a few of them actually suggested that their underlings take up the same gesture, saying, "From now on, instead of bowing to me, you might just touch my nose. It's a more refined and thoroughly modern custom."

In theory, the underlings wouldn't dare to reach their hands out and touch the noses of their higher-ups. But their bosses encouraged them with broad, beaming smiles, and so it began, with tentative touches, squeezes, and palpations of those superior schnozzolas, which turned shiny and red with satisfaction.

Giovannino hadn't forgotten his chief objective, which was to touch the nose of the king himself. He was just biding his time, waiting for the right moment. It finally came during a royal procession. Giovannino noticed that every so often, some member of the crowd rushed forward, climbed onto the steps of the monarch's carriage, and handed the king an envelope, certainly containing some plea or petition, which the king would pass with a smile to his prime minister.

When the carriage drew sufficiently near, Giovannino leapt onto the carriage step, and while the king flashed him an inviting smile, he said, "Pardon me," reached his arm out, and rubbed the tip of his finger on the tip of His Royal Highness's illustrious nose.

The king reached up and touched his nose, nonplussed, and opened his mouth as if to speak, but Giovannino, in the meantime, had leapt backward to safety, mingling with the crowd. A roar of applause burst forth, and other subjects immediately surged forward excitedly to imitate Giovannino's example: They leapt onto the carriage step, grabbed the king by the nose, and gave it a good hard shake.

"It's simply a new way of paying homage, Your Majesty," the prime minister murmured into the king's ear with a smile.

The king, however, didn't feel much like smiling. His nose was hurting, and it was also starting to run, and he hadn't even had a chance to wipe it, because his faithful subjects weren't giving him so much as a moment's respite and just kept cheerfully grabbing him by the nose.

Giovannino went home, pleased as punch.

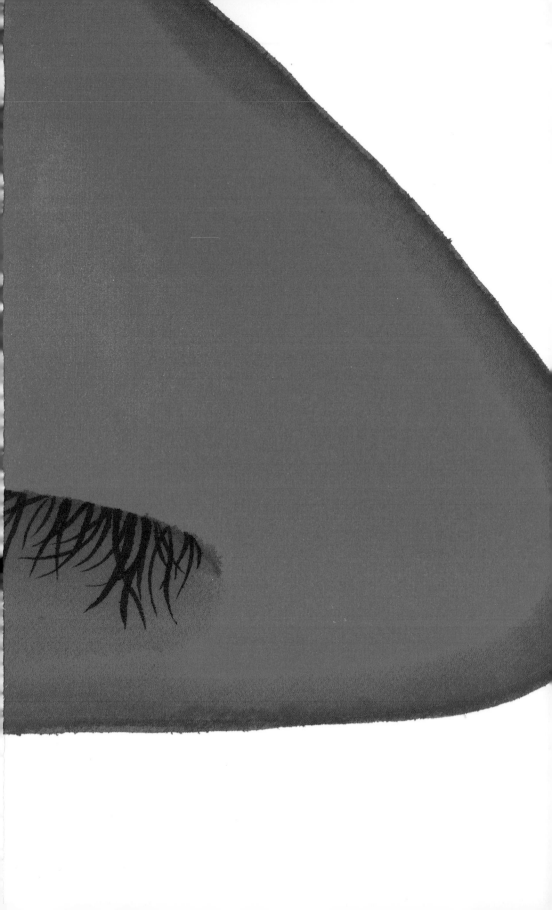

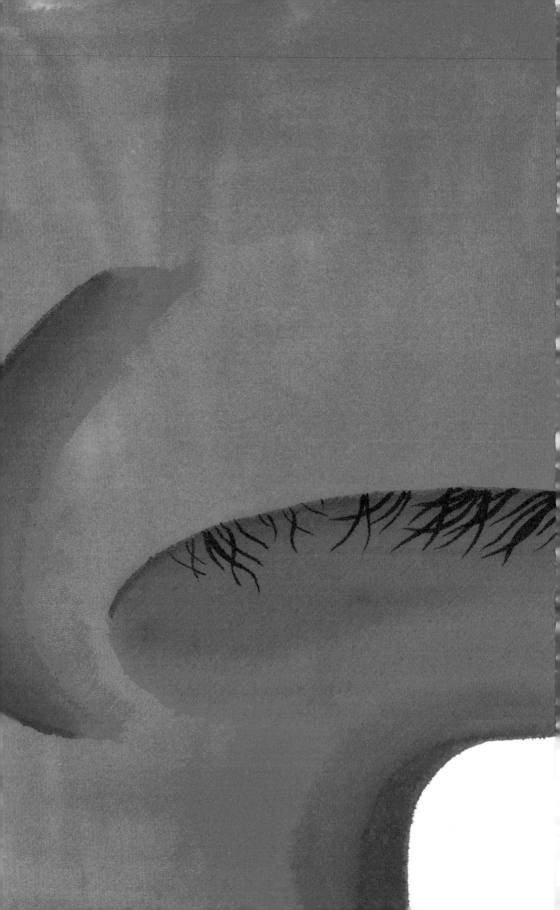

THE FAMOUS RAINSTORM OF PIOMBINO

Once upon a time, in the town of Piombino, it rained Jordan almonds. They came down as big as hailstones, but they were all different colors: green, pink, purple, blue. One little boy put a green nugget in his mouth, just to try it, and found that it tasted of mint. Another tasted a pink nugget and found it tasted of strawberry.

"It's raining Jordan almonds! It's raining Jordan almonds!"

Everyone hurried out into the streets to fill their pockets.

But there was no keeping up with the Jordan almonds; the downpour was just too heavy.

The rain didn't last long, but it left the streets covered with a sweet-smelling carpet that crunched underfoot. On their way home from school, the children found enough left to fill their book bags. Little old ladies put together very nice bundles with their headscarves.

It was a red-letter day.

And some people are still waiting for the next rainstorm of Jordan almonds, but that particular cloud has never passed over Piombino again, or over Turin, and it may never pass over Cremona.

THE MERRY-GO-ROUND OF CESENATICO

Once upon a time, in the beach town of Cesenatico, a traveling merry-go-round happened along. All told, it had six wooden horses, and six slightly faded red jeeps, for the children with more modern tastes. The little man who turned the merry-go-round with the strength of his arms was short and skinny, and he had the face of someone who probably eats only every other day, at best. In other words, it certainly wasn't much of a merry-go-round, but it attracted the children as if it were made of solid chocolate. The kids thronged around it, all agog, and whined and pouted to be treated to a ride.

What's so special about this merry-go-round? Is it made of honey? The mothers all wondered. Instead, they suggested to the children, "Let's go look at the dolphins in the canal. Let's go sit down at that café with the glider seats."

But the children wouldn't hear of it. All they wanted was the merry-go-round.

One evening, after setting his grandson down in one of the jeeps, an old man climbed onto the merry-go-round himself, settling into the saddle of a small wooden steed. He wasn't particularly comfortable, because his legs were too long, and his feet rested on the platform, which made him laugh. But as soon as the little man started spinning the merry-go-round, an astonishing thing happened: The old man suddenly found himself high atop the thirty-fifth floor of Cesenatico's famous skyscraper. His little wooden horse was galloping through the air, its muzzle straining straight up toward the clouds. He looked down and saw all of the Romagna region, and soon, all

52

of Italy below him, and then the whole wide world as it dwindled into the distance beneath his horse's hooves. Very soon, the Earth, too, was a small bright-blue merry-go-round that spun and spun, displaying the continents one after another and the oceans clearly sketched, as if on a geographic map.

Where can we be going? the old man wondered.

Just then, his little grandson sailed past him at the wheel of one of the old, red, slightly faded jeeps, now transformed into a spacecraft. And behind his grandson, in a long line, were all the other children, content and confident in their orbits.

He wondered where the little man who operated the merry-go-round would be by now. All the same, he could still hear the record playing its horrible cha-cha-cha. Every ride on the merry-go-round lasted one playing of the record.

So, there is a trick after all, the old man thought. *That little man must be a sorcerer.*

After which he thought, *If we can fly all the way around the world in the time it takes to play a record, then we'll beat the cosmonaut Yuri Gagarin's record.*

Now the space caravan was soaring over the Pacific Ocean with all its little islands—Australia, with its leaping kangaroos, and the South Pole, where millions of penguins stood peering up into the air, their beaks pointing skyward. But there was no time to count them, for soon North America was down below, with smoke signals lofting into the sky in the Southwest and the skyscrapers of New York.

Then, suddenly, there was just a single thirty-five-story skyscraper—the skyscraper of Cesenatico. The record had come to an end. The old man looked around in amazement. He was back on the old, peaceful merry-go-round on the shores of the Adriatic Sea, and the little man was slowing it to halt gently, without jerks or jolts.

The old man got off, his legs unsteady.

"Say, listen, you," he said to the little man.

But the man had no time to listen, as more children had jumped onto the horses and into the jeeps, and the merry-go-round was starting up for another trip around the world.

53

"Say," the old man repeated, a little annoyed by now.

But the little man didn't even bother to glance in his direction. He was moving the merry-go-round. Around and around went the laughing faces of the children, looking out to find their parents. And their parents, all in a circle, were gazing back at them, with smiles of encouragement on their lips.

Could the carousel operator really be a sorcerer? Could that silly machine spinning around to the tune of an annoying cha-cha-cha really be a magical merry-go-round?

Never mind, the old man decided. *I'd better not mention this to anyone. Perhaps they'd laugh behind my back and say to me,* "Don't you know at your age that it's dangerous to ride on a merry-go-round, because you might get dizzy?"

ON THE BEACH AT OSTIA

A few miles outside of Rome is the beach of Ostia, and in the summer, the Romans flock to it by the thousands, so that soon, there's not enough room on the beach to dig a hole in the sand with a plastic shovel. Whoever shows up last will have no idea where to set up their beach umbrella.

Once upon a time, a whimsical and most peculiar gentleman happened onto the beach of Ostia. Arriving last, he couldn't find anywhere in the sand to plant the beach umbrella under his arm. So, instead, he opened it up and fiddled around with the handle for a moment, and immediately, the umbrella rose into the air. It wafted over to the water's edge, hovering seven to eight feet above the tips of the other umbrellas. Then this industrious gentleman unfolded his lounge chair, and it, too, floated up into the air, and there, reclining in the shade of the umbrella, he pulled a book out of his pocket and started to read, taking deep breaths of the sea air, which sparkled with salt and iodine.

At first, no one even noticed him. They were sheltering under their own beach umbrellas, craning their necks to glimpse a tiny patch of water between the heads of all the other people in front of them, or else they were doing crossword puzzles. So no one was gazing up into the air. But then, out of the blue, a woman heard something fall onto her umbrella.

She guessed it was a ball and stepped out from under, ready to scold the children. But when she looked around and up, all she saw was the funny gentleman floating overhead.

The gentleman was looking down, and he said to the lady,

"Forgive me, signora. I dropped my book. Would you be so kind as to throw it back up to me?"

In her surprise, the woman fell down onto the sand in a sitting position, and since she was so hot and sweaty, she was unable to get back onto her feet. Her relatives came running to help her, and the lady, speechless, pointed up at the flying beach umbrella.

"Madame," the funny man said again, "would you please throw me up my book?"

"Hey, don't you see you scared our aunt?"

"I'm really quite sorry, but I certainly never meant to."

"Then come down from up there. It's against the rules."

"I most certainly will not! There was no room on the sand, so I decided to stay up here for a while. I pay taxes just like you, you know."

Meanwhile, all the Romans down on the beach seemed to have made up their minds to look up one after another, and they laughed as they pointed at the bizarre beachgoer.

"Would you take a look at that guy," they said. "He's got a rocket-propelled beach umbrella!"

"Hey, Yuri Gagarin!" they yelled at him. "You want to give me a ride too?"

A little boy tossed him up his book, and the gentleman started leafing through the pages with some signs of irritation, looking for his place. Then he resumed his reading, with a sigh of annoyance. Little by little, people drifted away, until he was finally left in peace. Only the children from time to time would look enviously up into the air, and the braver ones would call, "Mister, mister!"

"What is it?"

"Can you teach us how to float up in the air like you?"

But the man just heaved another sigh of annoyance and went back to his reading.

At sunset, with a faint swish, the beach umbrella took flight, and the funny man landed on the road, right next to his motorcycle, which he climbed onto and zoomed away. Who knows who he really was or where he bought that beach umbrella?

57

THE COMIC STRIP MOUSE

A comic strip mouse, tired of living in the pages of a newspaper and eager to replace the flavor of paper with the taste of cheese, took a great leap and found himself in the world of flesh and blood mice.

"Squash!" he exclaimed immediately, catching a whiff of the scent of cat.

"Beg your pardon?" whispered the other mice, intimidated by that strange new word.

"Sploom, bang, gulp!" said the little mouse, who spoke only the language of comic strips.

"He must be Turkish," ventured an old mouse who had traveled on freight ships and had worked the shipping routes of the Mediterranean before his retirement. But when he tried to speak to the mouse in Turkish, the comic strip mouse just looked at him in astonishment and said, "Ziip, fiiish, bonk."

"He's not Turkish," concluded the seafaring mouse. "But then what is he?"

"Beats me."

So they started calling him Beat Smee, and they treated him more or less like the village idiot.

"Hey, Beat Smee," they'd say, "which kind of cheese do you like best: Parmesan or Swiss?"

"Spliiit, grong, zizizíiir," the comic-strip mouse replied.

"Oh, good grief," laughed the other mice.

The littlest mice even pulled his tail on purpose to hear him object in that funny way of his: "Zoong, splash, squarr!"

60

Once, they all went hunting for food in a flour mill full of sacks of white flour and corn meal. The mice sank their teeth into that manna from heaven and chewed vigorously, making the sounds of crick, crack, crick, crack, just like all normal mice when they chew.

But the comic strip mouse went, "Crowck, scrowck, schrowck."

"At least you could try to eat like a civilized mouse," grumbled the seafaring mouse. "If we were aboard a freighter, you'd already have been thrown overboard. Whether or not you realize it, you make quite a disgusting noise."

"Crengh," said the comic strip mouse, and he dove back into a bag of corn.

With that, the seafaring mouse gestured discreetly to the others, and they very quietly tiptoed away, abandoning the stranger to his fate, certain that he'd never find his way back home.

For a while, the mouse went on chewing. By the time he finally realized he was alone, it was too dark to try to find his way back, so he decided to spend the night in the mill. He was just about to fall asleep when there, in the darkness, two yellow spotlights blinked on, followed by the sinister rustling of four predatory paws. A cat!

"Squash!" said the comic strip mouse with a shudder.

"Gragrragnau!" replied the cat.

Horrors! It was a comic-strip cat! The tribe of real cats had kicked him out because he didn't know how to say meow like a proper cat.

The two misfits embraced, swearing undying friendship, and they spent the rest of the night conversing in the strange language of comic strips. They understood each other to perfection.

HISTORY OF
THE KINGDOM
OF PIEHOLIA

In the ancient, distant land of Pieholia, to the east of the duchy of Gooddrink, Piehole the Great Digester reigned. He was the first of his name, so dubbed because after eating a bowl of spaghetti, he would gnaw away at the bowl, too, and digest it perfectly.

Succeeding him on the throne was Piehole the Second, better known as Three Soup Spoons, because when he ate soup, he used three silver soup spoons at a time. He held two himself, one in each hand, while the queen held the third—and woe betide Her Royal Highness if the third spoon wasn't kept full.

After him, in order of succession, the throne of Pieholia was occupied by the following monarchs, each of whom sat at the head of a heavily laden banqueting table, where the food was replenished day and night:

Piehole the Third, better known as Antipasto;

Piehole the Fourth, better known as Parmesan Cutlet;

Piehole the Fifth, the Ravenous;

Piehole the Sixth, the Turkey Ravager;

Piehole the Seventh, better known as Any More for Me?, who went so far as to devour his own crown, even though it was fashioned of wrought iron;

Piehole the Eighth, better known as Cheese Crust, who gobbled down the tablecloth when he found nothing more to eat on the table; and Piehole the Ninth, better known as Iron Jaws, who ate the throne with all the cushions.

And so the dynasty ended.

ALICE FALLS INTO THE SEA

Once, Alice Tumbledown went to the sea, fell in love with it, and never wanted to leave the water again.

"Alice, come out of the water!" her mother called.

"Right away! Here I come," Alice replied. But each time, what she was actually thinking was, *I'll stay in the water until fins grow out of my back and sides. Until I turn into a fish!*

At night, before going to bed, Alice would look at her back in the mirror to see whether fins were growing or at least a silvery scale or two. But all she could ever see were grains of sand, and that was only when she'd been careless with her scrubbing in the shower.

One morning, she went down to the beach earlier than usual, and there she met a boy who was gathering sea urchins and sunset shells. He was the son of local fisherfolk, and he knew all there was to know about the sea and everything in it.

"Do you know how to turn into a fish?" Alice asked him.

"I'll show you right now," the boy replied.

He set his handkerchief full of sea urchins and sunset shells down on a low rock and dove into the sea. A minute went by, two minutes went by … The boy didn't come back to the surface. But then, behold, in his place there appeared a dolphin, leaping and somersaulting over the waves and cheerfully splashing sprays of water into the air. The dolphin came and played between Alice's feet, and she felt absolutely no fear of it.

After a little while, with an elegant flip of its tail, the dolphin swam out into the open water. In the dolphin's place, the boy with the sunset shells reemerged from the water and smiled at her. "So, did you see how easy that was?"

"I saw, but I'm not sure I'd know how to do it myself."

"Give it a try."

Alice dove in, wishing with all her might to become a starfish, but instead she fell into the shell of a giant mollusk just as it was yawning, and it immediately snapped shut its valves, imprisoning Alice and all her dreams.

Here I am, in trouble again, thought Alice. But she also felt what silence—what fresh, cool peace—was there inside the giant mollusk. It would have been wonderful to stay there forever and to live on the seabed like the mermaids in days of old. Alice sighed. She thought of her mother, who was sure Alice was still fast asleep in her bed. She thought of her father, who was expected from the city that very morning, since it was Saturday.

"I can't abandon them," she told herself. "They love me too much. I'll return back to shore this one time."

By bracing her feet and her hands, Alice managed to pry the seashell open sufficiently to leap out and float to the surface. The sea-urchin boy was already far away, and Alice never told anyone about what happened to her that night.

THE WAR
OF THE BELLS

Once upon a time, there was a war—a great and terrible war—in which vast numbers of soldiers died on both sides. We were on this side, and our enemies were on the other, and we shot at each other day and night, but the war went on so long that finally, there was no more bronze to make cannons, no more iron to make bayonets, and on it went.

Our commander in chief, Mega General Bombardier Big Guns della Earsplitter, gave the order to remove all the bells from all the belfries and to melt them all down in order to cast an enormous cannon—just one, but one big enough to win the whole war with a single shot.

It took a hundred thousand cranes to lift that cannon; it took ninety-seven trains to transport it to the front. The Mega General rubbed his hands together in delight and said, "When my cannon fires, our enemies will run away all the way to the moon."

The great moment arrived. The super cannon was aimed at the enemy. We'd all stuffed cotton wads into our ears, because the blast was perfectly capable of shattering our eardrums and our eustachian tubes.

The Mega General Bombardier Big Guns della Earsplitter ordered, "Fire!"

An artilleryman pushed a button. Suddenly, from one end of the front to the other, came the gigantic sound of pealing bells: *Ding! Dong! Bong!*

We took the cotton out of our ears to be able to hear it more clearly.

Ding! Dong! Bong! thundered the super cannon. And a hundred thousand echoes carried the sound over mountains and across valleys: *Ding! Dong! Bong!*

"Fire!" shouted the Mega General a second time. "Fire, confound you!"

The artilleryman pressed the button once again, and again a festive concert of bells spread through the trenches. It sounded as if all the bells in the nation were pealing all at once. In a fit of rage, the Mega General was tearing his hair out, and he went right on tearing it out until only one hair remained.

Then there was a moment of silence. And from the other side of the battle line, as if by some signal, there came in response a cheerful, deafening *Ding! Dong! Bong!*

Because you need to know that the enemy commander, Feldmarschall von Bombardieren Großen Gunnen und Earschplitteren, had also come up with the idea of manufacturing a super cannon by melting down all the bells in his country.

Ding! Bong! our cannon now thundered.

Dong! replied the enemy cannon. And the soldiers of both armies leapt out of the trenches and ran to embrace each other, dancing and shouting, "The bells! The bells! Let's celebrate! Peace has broken out!"

The Mega General and the Feldmarschall each climbed into his car and raced far, far away until each had run out of gas, but the sound of the bells pursued them still.

THE YOUNG CRAYFISH

A young crayfish wondered, *Why does everyone in my family walk backward? I want to learn how to walk forward, just like frogs, and may my tail fall off if I fail.*

He started practicing secretly among the pebbles of his home stream, and for the first few days, the undertaking cost him a tremendous effort. He knocked into everything, he dented his carapace, and he crushed one foot with another. But little by little, things started going better, because you can learn anything if you set your mind to it.

When he was confident of his abilities, he went to his family and said, "Watch this, everybody."

And he broke into a magnificent, if short, forward run.

"Oh, my son," his mother said, bursting into tears. "Have you lost your mind? Come to your senses—walk the way your father and mother taught you, walk like your brothers and sisters who love you so dearly."

But his brothers and sisters just couldn't stop snickering.

His father stood there watching him for a while, then said, "Enough's enough. If you want to go on living with us, walk like all the other crayfish. If you want to be headstrong and do as you please, well, the stream runs for miles. Begone, and never come back."

The good young crayfish loved his family, but his certainty was stronger than any doubts he had. So he hugged his mother, said farewell to his father and brothers, and went out into the great, big world.

When he walked by a group of frogs that had gathered on

68

a lily pad to gossip like the good housewives that they were, they couldn't help but notice.

"The world has turned upside down," said one of the frogs. "Take a look at that crayfish and tell me if I'm wrong."

"The young have no more respect for their elders," chimed in another frog.

"Oh me, oh my," chorused a third.

But the young crayfish continued on his way—following his nose, we might safely say, given the fact that he was walking forward. At some point, he heard an elderly crayfish who was sitting all alone by a rock with a sad expression on his face talking to him.

"Hello," replied the young crayfish.

The elderly crayfish observed him for a long time, and then said, "What do you think you're doing? When I was a young crayfish, I also thought I could teach the other crayfish to walk facing forward. And look what good it did me—I live all alone now, and people would sooner bite their tongue off than actually speak to me. You're still in time, take my word for it: Resign yourself to doing as everyone else does, and someday, you'll thank me for this advice."

The young crayfish didn't know how to respond, so he fell silent. Inwardly, however, he thought, *I still know I'm right.*

He very politely said goodbye to the elderly crayfish and proudly went right on his way.

Will he go far? Will he make his fortune? Will he right all the wrongs of this world? We have no way of knowing, because he's still marching along with all the courage and determination of the very first day he set out. We can only wish him a very good journey, with all our heart: "Buon viaggio! Safe travels, young crayfish!"

THE GIANT'S HAIR

Once upon a time, there were four brothers. Three were very small but also very clever, while the fourth brother was a giant—immensely powerful, but nowhere near as clever as his brothers.

His strength was in his hands and his arms, but his intelligence was in his hair. So his clever little brothers kept his hair very short, to make sure that he was always a little dopey. Then, they could make him do all the hard work, since he was so strong. For their own part, they just loitered about, pocketing all his earnings.

They made him plow the fields, they made him split the wood, turn the mill wheel, and haul the cart in place of the horse. As he hauled the cart, his sly smaller brothers sat on the coachman's seat and drove him onward with cracks of the whip.

And while they sat on the coachman's seat, they kept their eyes on his head, telling him: "You look so good with short hair."

"True beauty doesn't consist of curly locks."

"Look at that tuft growing out! We'll have to get out the scissors this evening."

As they talked, they exchanged winks and elbowed each other cheerfully in the ribs. At the market, they'd pocket their earnings, go to the tavern, and leave the giant behind to stand guard over the cart.

They gave him only enough food to ensure he was strong enough to work, and they gave him only so much drink as his

thirst demanded—and only the kind of wine you get from a well (i.e., water).

One day, the giant fell sick. His smaller brothers, afraid he might die while still able to work, sent for the finest doctors in the land. They gave him the costliest medicines to drink. They served him breakfast in bed.

They fluffed up his pillows and tucked him comfortably into bed, telling him all the while, "You see how we love you? So, don't die on us now. Don't do us wrong."

They were so worried about their brother's health that they forgot to keep an eye on his hair. His locks had all the time in the world to grow longer than they ever had before, and as his hair grew, the giant's intelligence grew back to its normal size. He began to think about things, to observe his little brothers carefully, to add up two plus two and four plus four.

He finally realized just how diabolical they had been and what a fool he'd been to fall for their tricks. Right then and there, though, he was careful to say nothing. He waited until he had regained his strength, and one morning, while his little brothers were still sleeping, he got up early, trussed them up like so many salamis, and loaded them onto the cart.

"Where are you taking us, brother dear? Where are you taking your beloved little brothers?"

"Oh, you'll see."

He took them to the station and put them on the train, tied up tight just as they were, and his only farewell to them was this: "Go, and never show your faces again in this part of the world. You've tricked me once too often. Now I'm the master."

The engine whistled, the wheels turned, and the three sly brothers lay there, just as good as could be. In fact, no one ever saw them again.

THE NOSE
THAT RAN AWAY

Nikolai Gogol told the story of a nose that roamed freely around Leningrad, taking rides in carriages and getting up to all sorts of antics.

A similar story actually happened in Laveno on Lake Maggiore. One morning, a gentleman who lived right across from the wharf, where the ferryboats come and go, got out of bed, went into the bathroom for his morning shave, took one look in the mirror, and shouted, "Help! My nose!"

In the middle of his face, where his nose belonged, there was nothing at all, just a smooth patch of skin. The gentleman ran out onto the balcony, still in his bathrobe, just in time to see his nose rush out onto the town piazza and then head off at a rapid clip toward the landing dock, squeezing past the cars that were boarding the ferry for Verbania.

"Stop! Stop!" shouted the man. "My nose! Stop! Thief, thief!"

People looked up at him and laughed. "So, someone stole your nose and left you that mug? You certainly got the short end of the stick."

The gentleman had no choice but to hurry downstairs and chase after the runaway nose, all the while holding a handkerchief in front of his face, as if he had a cold. Unfortunately, he got to the landing dock, just as the ferryboat was pulling away. The gentleman leapt courageously into the water and swam after the ferry as passengers and tourists shouted, "Go for it! You can do it!" But the ferryboat had already picked up speed, and the captain had no intention of heading back to pick up late arrivals.

"You can just wait for the next ferry!" a sailor shouted at the gentleman. "They come every half hour!"

The gentleman, crestfallen, was walking back up to the shore when he suddenly spied his nose. Having spread a cloak on the water, like St. Julius in the legend, the nose was moving across the lake at moderate speed.

"So, you didn't take the ferry after all? It was all just a ruse?!" the man shouted at his nose.

The nose continued looking straight ahead, like an old pilot dog, and didn't even bother to look around. The cloak beneath it undulated gently like a jellyfish.

"Where are you going?!" shouted the man.

Steadfast, the nose gave no response, and its unfortunate owner resignedly swam back to the port of Laveno. To return home, he had no choice but to walk through a crowd of rubberneckers.

He went upstairs and shut himself in, giving orders to his housekeeper that he was home to no one. He spent the next few days looking at his noseless face in the mirror.

A few days later, a fisherman from Ranco pulled up his nets and found the runaway nose, which had sunk in the middle of the lake because the cloak was full of holes. He decided to take the nose to the market in Laveno.

The gentleman's housekeeper, who had gone down to the market to buy some fish for dinner, immediately spotted the nose laid out for sale amidst the carp and pikes.

"Why, that's my employer's nose!" she exclaimed, aghast. "Give it to me right away so I can take it to him."

"I have no idea who it belongs to," said the fisherman, "but I caught it, and I'm selling it."

"For how much?"

"For its weight in gold, of course. It's a nose; it's not just some lake perch."

The housekeeper ran home to inform her employer.

"Give him whatever he asks! I want my nose back!"

The housekeeper realized that it would cost a lot of money, because that nose was a pretty big one. In fact, it cost

78

tremendeen thousand lire, eleventy-thirty and a half. In order to raise the sum, she was even forced to sell her earrings, but because she was very fond of her master, she sacrificed them with a sigh.

She bought the nose, wrapped it in a handkerchief, and took it home. The nose let itself be conveyed without a hint of trouble, and it didn't even rebel when its owner greeted it with trembling hands.

"But why did you run away in the first place? What did I ever do to you?"

The nose glared at him, wrinkling all over in disgust, and said, "Listen, just never pick me again as long as you live. Or if you do, at least clip your nails."

THE ROAD TO NOWHERE

At the edge of town, there was a fork in the road. One road went down toward the sea, the other went toward the city, and the third led nowhere at all.

Martino knew this because he'd asked just about everyone, and everyone had given him the same reply: "That third road? It doesn't go anywhere. It's pointless to take it."

"But how far does it go?"

"It doesn't go anywhere."

"Then why did they build it?"

"Nobody built it. It's always been there."

"But hasn't anybody ever taken it to see where it goes?"

"You sure are hardheaded. We just told you that there's nothing worth seeing …"

"But how can you be sure, if you've never taken it?" He was so obstinate that people started calling him Martino Hardhead, but he didn't mind. He just kept thinking about the road that went nowhere.

When he was old enough to cross the street without holding his grandfather's hand, he got up early one morning, left the town, and without a moment's hesitation set off down the mysterious road, and kept right on going. The surface was riddled with potholes and weeds, but luckily it hadn't rained in quite a while, so there were no puddles. A hedge extended along both sides of the road, but soon the woods began. The tree branches intertwined overheard, creating a cool, dark corridor, penetrated by the occasional shaft of sunlight, which lit his way.

Martino walked and walked, the tunnel went on and on, and the road, too, went on and on. His feet were starting to ache. He was already wondering if he shouldn't turn back when he saw a dog.

"Where there's a dog, there's a house," Martino told himself, "or at least a person."

The dog ran toward him, wagging its tail and licking Martino's hands. Then it turned and headed off down the road, turning around every so often to make sure that Martino was still following.

"I'm coming! I'm coming!" Martino called out, his curiosity piqued. At last, the forest started to thin out, the sky could be seen high above, and the road came to an end at the threshold of a large wrought-iron gate.

Through the bars, Martino glimpsed a castle with all its doors and windows thrown wide open. Smoke plumed up out of all the chimneys, and from a high balcony, a lovely lady was waving to him and crying cheerfully, "Come in! Come right in, Martino Hardhead!"

"Well, well, well," Martino told himself cheerfully, "I never knew I'd get here, but I certainly did!"

He pushed open the gate, strode across the grounds, and walked into the great room of the castle just in time to make a deep bow to the lovely lady as she descended the monumental staircase. She was beautiful, and she was dressed even better than fairies and princesses. What's more, she was quite cheerful, and she laughed as she said, "So you didn't believe it."

"Didn't believe what?"

"What everyone told you about the road going nowhere."

"It just made no sense. And if you ask me, there are even more places in the world than there are roads."

"Of course there are, as long as you're willing to get up and go see them. Come on in. Let me show you around the castle."

There were more than a hundred drawing rooms, all packed with treasures of every kind, like those castles in fairy tales where sleeping beauties slumber or ogres pile up riches.

There were diamonds, precious gems, gold, and silver. And the whole time, the lovely lady kept saying, "Take what you want—take whatever you want. I'll lend you a cart to take it home, it will be so heavy."

As you can imagine, Martino didn't have to be told twice.

The cart was piled high when he finally left. Sitting with paws around the reins was the dog, who was well-trained and knew how to jerk the reins and bark at the horses when they dozed and wandered off the road.

Back in town, where he'd already been given up for dead, Martino Hardhead was greeted with immense astonishment.

The dog unloaded all Martino's treasures in the town square, wagged its tail twice in farewell, climbed back onto the cart, and drove off in a cloud of dust. Martino gave generous gifts to one and all—both friends and enemies—and was made to tell the tale of his adventure a hundred times over. Every time he finished the story, another member of his audience would hurry home, get out a cart and horse, and rush off down the road that led nowhere.

But that same evening, they all came trailing back, one after the other, with long faces and crushed spirits. For them, the road ended in the middle of the forest, smack up against a dense wall of trees in a sea of thorns. There was no more gate, no more castle, no lovely lady. Because certain treasures are there only for the first to blaze a new trail, and the first had been Martino Hardhead.

THE SCARECROW

Gonario was the youngest of seven brothers. His parents had no money to provide him with an education, so they sent him off to work on a large farm. Gonario's job was being a scarecrow, to keep birds away from the fields. Every morning, he was given a paper wrapper full of gunpowder, and for hours and hours, Gonario would walk back and forth across the fields, stopping every so often to set fire to a pinch of gunpowder. The explosions startled the birds and sent them fluttering, in fear of hunters.

Once, the gunpowder set Gonario's jacket on fire, and if the boy hadn't had the presence of mind to leap into an irrigation ditch, he certainly would have burnt to death. His dive frightened the frogs, and they hopped away quickly, with a great deal of croaking. All that croaking, in turn, scared the crickets, which stopped chirping for a moment.

But none of them were as frightened as Gonario himself, who stood weeping all alone on the banks of the irrigation ditch, drenched like an ugly duckling, looking small, ragged, and hungry. He was sobbing so bitterly that a flock of crows landed on the branches of a tree to watch him. They cawed compassionately to comfort him. But crows can't comfort a scarecrow.

This story took place in Sardinia.

PLAYING WITH
THE CANE

One day, little Claudio was playing just inside the front door of his apartment building when he saw a nice little old man go by out on the street. The old man wore gold wire-rim glasses, and he was walking completely hunched over, leaning his weight on his cane. Right in front of Claudio's door, the old man suddenly lost hold of his cane.

Claudio hurried out to pick it up and hand it to him, but the old man smiled and said, "Thanks, but I don't need it. I can walk just fine without one. If you like, you can keep it."

And without stopping to wait for an answer, he started off, his back looking less curved than before.

Claudio stood there with the walking stick in his hands, unsure of what to do with it. It was just a perfectly ordinary cane, with a curved handle and a metal tip—nothing special about it worth mentioning.

Claudio knocked the tip against the ground two or three times, and then, almost without thinking about it, he leaned the cane forward and straddled it. Lo and behold, it was no longer an ordinary cane. It was now a horse—a wonderful black colt with a white star on its forehead—and it burst into a gallop around the courtyard, whinnying and kicking sprays of fiery sparks off the cobblestones.

Once Claudio, who was astonished and a little frightened, managed to get his feet back on solid ground, the walking stick turned back into a walking stick. It no longer had hooves, just a simple, slightly rusty metal tip; it no longer had a flowing mane, just the usual curved handle.

I want to try that again, Claudio decided after catching his breath.

He swung his leg over the cane again, and this time it became, not a horse, but a very solemn two-humped camel, and the courtyard was now a vast desert to be crossed. This time, Claudio wasn't a bit afraid, and he peered off into the distance, waiting for an oasis to heave into view.

This is certainly an enchanted cane, Claudio thought as he climbed onto it for a third time. Now it was a bright-red race car with its number written in white on the hood, and the courtyard was a roaring race track, and Claudio was the first across the finish line every time.

Then the cane turned into a speedboat, and the courtyard turned into a lake with placid, green waters, and then a spaceship hurtling through space, leaving a wake of stars behind it.

Each time Claudio set foot on the ground again, the walking stick returned to its ordinary appearance, with a shiny handle and a worn, old metal tip.

The afternoon passed quickly as the boy played those games. As evening began to fall, Claudio chanced to look back out onto the street, and there was the old man with the gold wire-rim glasses again. Claudio gazed at him curiously,

but he couldn't see anything remarkable about him—he was just an ordinary old man, looking a little weary from his long walk.

"Do you like the cane?" the old man asked Claudio with a smile.

Claudio thought the old man must want it back, and he held it out to him, slightly red-faced.

But the old man shook his head. "Keep it, keep it," he said. "What am I going to do with a cane, anyway, at my age? You can fly on it; I can only lean my weight on it. I'll lean against the wall instead, and it will make no difference."

And he walked off with a smile on his face, because no one in the world can be happier than an old person who has given a gift to a child.

OLD PROVERBS

"All cats are gray in the dark," decreed an old proverb.

"Actually, I'm black," announced a black cat as he crossed the street.

"That's impossible. Old proverbs are always right."

"That may be, but I'm still black," the cat insisted.

In an outburst of surprise and bitter disappointment, the old proverb fell off the roof and broke a leg.

Another old proverb went to the stadium to watch a soccer match. He took a player aside and whispered in his ear, "If you want something done right, do it yourself!"

The soccer player tried playing the ball all by himself, but the resulting play was unbelievably boring, and he never came close to winning, so he soon rejoined his team.

Crestfallen, the old proverb fell ill and had to have his tonsils removed.

Once, three old proverbs got together, and the minute they started talking, the conversation degenerated into an argument.

"Well begun is half done," said the first one.

"Not so, not so," said the second proverb. "The truth always lies somewhere in the middle."

"You're badly mistaken!" exclaimed the third. "Always save the best for last."

They started yanking each other's hair, and they're still going at it now.

Then there's the story of the old proverb who wanted to eat a pear so he went to wait under the tree. As he waited, he thought, *When the pear is ripe, it will fall*.

But when the pear finally did fall, it was completely gooey and rotten, and it splatted right on the old proverb's noggin. The old proverb was so mortified that he turned in his resignation.

APOLLONIA
THE JAM MAKER

In the town of Sant'Antonio on Lake Maggiore, there lived a little old woman who was very good at making jam—so good that her services were sought after in Valcuvia, in Valtravaglia, in Val Dumentina, and in Val Poverina. When it was jam season, people came from all the different mountain valleys, sat on the low stone wall, looked out at the view over the lake, picked a few raspberries from the raspberry bushes, and then called out to the famous little old jam maker, "Apollonia!"

"What is it?"

"Would you make me a pot of blueberry jam?"

"At your service."

"Would you help me make a nice plum jam?"

"Right away."

Apollonia, that little old lady, really did have golden fingers, and she made the finest jams in the Varese area and in all of the Canton Ticino.

One time, an old woman from Arcumeggia came to see her. That woman was so poor that she didn't have so much as a paper wrapper of peach pits to make the jam with, and so along the way, she had filled her apron with chestnut husks. "Apollonia, would you make me a pot of jam?"

"With chestnut husks?"

"I couldn't find anything else …"

"Oh well, let me try."

Apollonia did her best, and in the end, she made the finest jam imaginable out of chestnut husks.

Another time, that same woman from Arcumeggia couldn't even find chestnut husks, because when the dry leaves fell, they'd covered them up, so this time she arrived with an apronful of stinging nettles. "Apollonia, would you make me a pot of jam?"

"With stinging nettles?"

"I couldn't find anything else …"

"Oh well, we'll see how it turns out."

Apollonia took the bag of stinging nettles, poured plenty of sugar over them, boiled them the way only she knew how, and made a jam out of them that was finger-licking delicious.

Because Apollonia, that little old lady, had fingers of gold and silver, and she could have made a fine jam out of rocks.

One time, the emperor himself came through and insisted on tasting some of Apollonia's jam. She gave him a bowlful, but after the first spoonful, the emperor stopped eating in disgust, because a fly had fallen into it.

"This is disgusting," said the emperor.

"If the jam was no good, that fly would never have fallen into it in the first place," replied Apollonia.

But by now the emperor had lost his temper, and he ordered his soldiers to cut off Apollonia's hands.

At that, the people rose up in rebellion and told the emperor that if he had Apollonia's hands cut off, then there'd be nothing for it but to chop his crown off—and his head with it, because they could find heads to serve as emperor on any street corner, but golden hands like Apollonia's were far more rare and precious

And the emperor was forced to pack his bags and run away.

OLD AUNT ADA

When old aunt Ada was very aged indeed, she went to live in the old people's home, in a little room with three beds, where two other little old ladies already lived—every bit as old as she was. Old aunt Ada immediately sat down in a little chair by the window and crumbled a stale cookie onto the window-sill.

"Oh, how smart," said the other two little old women sarcastically. "That way, we'll get ants."

But instead, a little bird flew in from the garden of the old people's home, hungrily pecked at the cookie, and flew away.

"There, you see," grumbled the little old ladies. "What have you got to show for it? That bird pecked at the cookie and then flew away. Just like our children, who've gone out and traveled the world, and who even knows where they are now? They never think about us, who raised them."

Old aunt Ada said nothing, but every morning she crumbled a cookie on the windowsill, and the little bird always came to peck at it, always at the same time, as punctual as a pensioner. If the cookie wasn't ready yet, you just had to see how angry the little bird would get.

Time passed, and now the little bird would come with her young, because she'd made a nest and had hatched four eggs, and the little ones, too, pecked hungrily at old aunt Ada's cookie. The bird family came every morning, and if the cookie wasn't waiting for them, they'd kick up a tremendous ruckus.

"Your birdies are here," the little old women would say to old aunt Ada with a hint of envy. And Ada would run, so

to speak, with tiny steps to her dresser and pull out a stale cookie from between her packet of coffee and the pack of licorice candy, and as she did, she'd say, "Hold on, hold on! I'm coming."

"Eh," murmured the other little old ladies, "if only all it took was a cookie on the windowsill to bring back our children to us. What about your children, Aunt Ada? Where are your boys?"

Old aunt Ada didn't even know anymore—maybe in Austria, maybe in Australia—but she didn't allow herself to be distracted. She crumbled the cookie for her little birds and told them, "Come on, eat, eat. Otherwise, you won't have the strength to fly, to leave the nest."

And when they were done pecking at the cookie, she said, "Go on, fly away, fly away. What else are you waiting for? Your wings were made for flying."

The little old ladies shook their heads and decided that old aunt Ada must be a bit mad. Even as elderly and poor as she was, she still always had something to give away and never even expected anyone to say thank you.

Then old aunt Ada died, and her children only found out about it sometime later, when it was no longer worth their trouble to get tickets and travel for the funeral. But the little birds came back to the windowsill all winter long, protesting loudly because old aunt Ada hadn't crumbled their cookie for them.

THE SUN
AND THE CLOUD

The sun was riding across the sky, cheerful and glorious in his chariot of fire, casting his rays in all directions, to the immense displeasure of a cloud in a stormy mood, which muttered, "Squanderer. Wasteful fool. Go on and spend your rays, your sunshine. You'll see how much you have later."

In the vineyards, every grape ripening on the vine stole a ray or two every minute, and there wasn't a blade of grass or a spider or a flower or a drop of water that didn't take their share.

"Go on, let them rob you blind—you'll see how they thank you later, when you have nothing left to steal."

The sun went on his way, riding cheerfully through the sky, giving rays of sunshine away freely by the millions, by the billions, without bothering to count them.

It wasn't until sunset that he even bothered to count how many rays he had left, and surprise, surprise—he wasn't missing a single one. The cloud, astonished, dissolved into a sheet of hail, while the sun settled down happily into the sea.

THE KING
WHO WAS GOING
TO DIE

Once upon a time, a king was going to die. He was a very powerful king, but he was fatally ill, and he despaired at the thought. "Can it be that such a powerful king has to die? What are my sorcerers doing? Why don't they save me?"

But his sorcerers had all run away for fear of having their heads chopped off. Only one had remained—an old sorcerer to whom no one even listened anymore, because he was quite eccentric and perhaps even a bit mad. For many years now, the king had ignored him, but now he summoned him for a sorcery consultation.

"You can save yourself," said the sorcerer, "but on one condition: for one whole day you must give your throne to the man in your kingdom who most resembles you. Then that man will die in your place."

A proclamation went forth throughout the land: "All those who resemble the king are to present themselves at court within twenty-four hours, on pain of death."

A great many showed up. Some had a beard just like the king's, but a nose that was just a hint longer or shorter, and the sorcerer rejected them. Others resembled the king the way one orange resembles another in a crate at the fruit vendor's shop, but the sorcerer rejected them because they were missing a tooth or because they had a mole on their back.

"But you're rejecting them all," the king protested to the sorcerer. "Let me just try with one of them for starters."

"It won't do you a bit of good," the sorcerer retorted.

One evening, the king and his sorcerer were strolling on

the bastions of the city. Suddenly, the sorcerer shouted out, "There he is! The man who resembles you more than anyone else!"

So saying, he pointed to a lame, hunchbacked beggar, half-blind, dirty, and covered with scabs.

"But how can you say such a thing?" the king objected. "We have nothing in common."

"A king who is going to die," the sorcerer insisted, "alone resembles the poorest, most unfortunate man in the city. Hurry! Exchange your clothing for his, put him on the throne for a day, and your life will be saved."

But the king absolutely refused to admit that he resembled that beggar in the slightest, and he returned to the palace with a sulky expression. That same evening, he died with his crown on his head and his scepter in his hand.

THE COMET SORCERER

Once upon a time, a sorcerer invented a machine that made comets. It slightly resembled his machine for slicing soup, but it wasn't the same. Instead, it made comets to order—large or small, as you preferred, with single or double tails, casting a yellow light or a red, and so on and so forth.

The sorcerer roamed through city and town, never missed a single market, and even came to the Milan Trade Fair and the Horse Fair of Verona. Everywhere he went, he explained his machine and showed how easy it was to use. The comets would come out small with a string attached to hold them, and then, as they gradually rose into the air, they would grow to the size desired. Even the biggest comets were no harder to handle than a kite on a string.

People crowded around the sorcerer—the way people always crowd around anyone who shows off a machine at the market, whether it's a machine to make the thinnest spaghetti or peel potatoes—but they never once bought even the tiniest little comet.

"If it were a balloon, then maybe," said one good woman. "But if I buy my little boy a comet, who knows what kind of trouble he'll get up to?"

And the sorcerer replied, "Come now, give it some thought! Your children are going to travel to the stars. Start getting them used to it when they're still small."

"No, no, thanks. Someone else will travel to the stars, certainly not my son."

"Comets! Genuine comets for sale! Who wants a comet?"

102

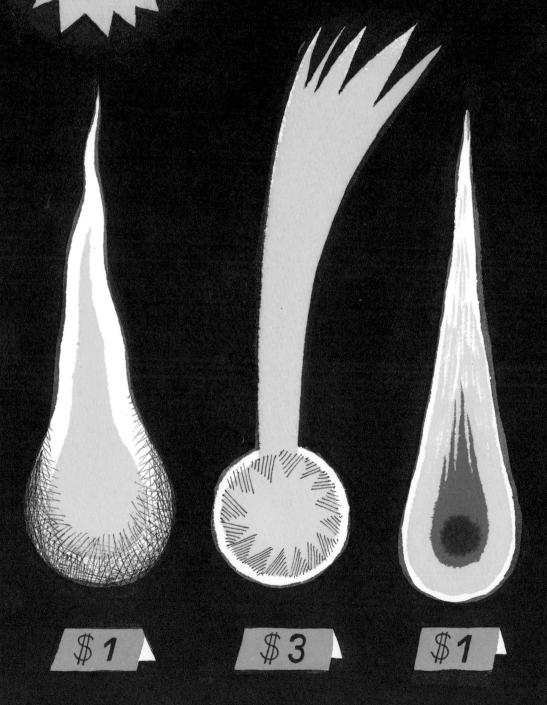

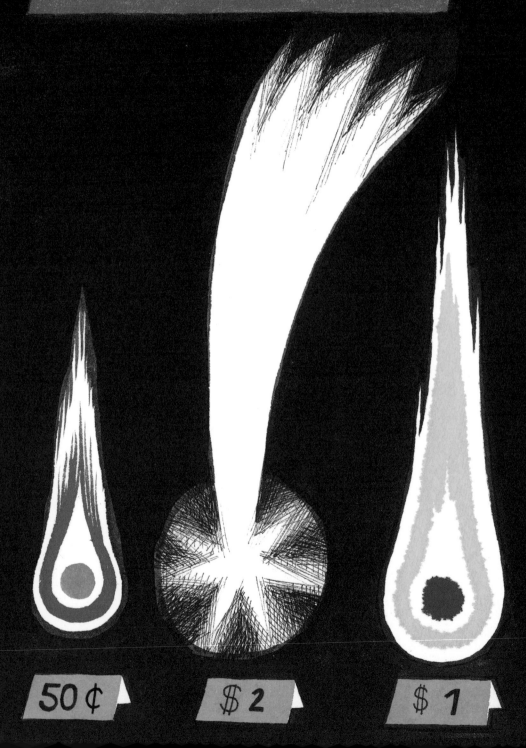

But no one wanted a comet.

The poor sorcere! With all the meals he had missed—because he never earned a penny—had withered away to skin and bones. And so one evening, when he was hungrier than usual, he transformed his comet-making machine into a nice Tuscan caciottella cheese and gobbled it down.

THE FISHERMAN OF CEFALŪ

Once upon a time, a fisherman from Cefalù was pulling his nets into his boat, and they felt so horribly heavy that he wondered what he was about to haul in. But all he found was a tiny little fish the length of his pinky. He grabbed it angrily and was about to throw it back into the water, when he heard a tiny little voice say, "Ouch! Don't squeeze me so hard."

The fisherman looked around and saw no one, neither near nor far, and he raised his arm to throw the fish back into the water, but then he heard the tiny voice again: "Don't throw me back! Don't throw me back!"

It was then that he realized that the voice was coming from the fish. He cut it open and inside he found a tiny, perfectly formed, little child, with feet, hands, and face all exactly as they ought to be, except for one thing—behind his back, the child had two fins, just like a fish.

"Who are you?"

"I'm the sea child."

"And what do you want with me?"

"If you keep me with you, I'll bring you good luck."

The fisherman heaved a sigh. "I already have so many children to feed. I would be the one to have this piece of luck—another mouth to feed."

"You'll see," said the sea child.

The fisherman took the sea child home, had a little smock made to hide his fins, and put him in the cradle his last-born child had occupied. The sea child didn't even cover half a pillow with his whole body.

But the amount of food he ate was alarming. He ate more than all the fisherman's children combined—and there were seven of them, each more ravenous than the next.

"What a piece of good luck, indeed," sighed the fisherman.

"Shall we go fishing?" asked the sea child the next morning, in his faint, piping voice.

They went out fishing, and the sea child said, "Row straight ahead until I tell you to stop. All right, here we are. Cast your nets here."

The fisherman did as he was told, and when he pulled the nets back in, he saw they were full like he'd never seen them before, and it was all fish of the finest quality.

The sea child clapped his hands. "I told you—I know where to find fish."

In a short while, the fisherman became rich, bought a second boat, and then a third, and then a great many, and all those boats went out on the sea to cast nets for him. All the nets were soon filled with the finest fish, and the fisherman earned so much money that he had to send one of his sons to study accounting, so he could keep track of it for the fisherman.

But as he became rich, the fisherman forgot how he had suffered when he was still poor. He treated his sailors badly, he paid them poorly, and if they complained, he fired them.

"How will we be able to feed our children?" they complained.

"Give them stones to eat," he told them. "You'll see—they'll digest them."

The sea child, who saw everything and heard everything, told him one evening, "Beware—what has been done can be undone."

But the fisherman just laughed at him and paid him no mind. Then, he took the sea child, shut him up in a big seashell, and threw him in the sea.

Who knows how long it will be before the sea child can get free? What would YOU do if you were he?

KING MIDAS

King Midas was a tremendous spendthrift. Every night, he threw parties and held balls until he no longer had a cent to his name. He went to see the sorcerer Apollo and told him his problems, so Apollo cast the following spell: "Anything your hands touch will turn to gold."

King Midas jumped for joy and went running back to his car, but no sooner had he touched the door handle, then the whole car turned to gold: gold wheels, gold windows, gold engine. The gasoline had turned to gold, too, so the car no longer ran, and he had to send for an ox-drawn cart to transport it.

As soon as he was home, King Midas went through all the rooms, touching as many things as he could—tables, armoires, chairs—and they all turned to gold. After a while, he felt thirsty, so he sent for a glass of water, but the glass turned to gold and so did the water, and if he wanted to drink, he had to let his servant spoon the liquid into his mouth.

Dinnertime came. He took his fork, and it turned to gold, and all the guests applauded and said, "Your Majesty, touch the buttons on my jacket, touch this umbrella."

King Midas did as they asked, but when he picked up the bread to bite into it, it, too, turned to gold, and if he wanted to satisfy his appetite, he had to let the queen spoon-feed him. The guests all ducked under the table to laugh at him, infuriating King Midas. He grabbed one of the guests and turned his nose to gold, so that the man could no longer blow it.

Then it was time for bed, but King Midas accidentally touched his pillow, the sheets, and the mattress, and they,

110

too, turned to gold, which was too uncomfortable to sleep on. So, he spent the night in an armchair with both arms raised to ensure he touched nothing. The next morning, dead tired, he went galloping back to the sorcerer Apollo and asked him to undo the spell, and Apollo did as he was asked.

"All right," Apollo told him, "but pay close attention, because it will take exactly seven hours and seven minutes before the spell can be undone, and during that time, anything you touch will turn into cow manure."

King Midas went away much comforted, and he paid close attention to the clock, making sure he touched nothing before seven hours and seven minutes had passed.

Unfortunately, his clock ran just a little fast, gaining a minute every hour. When it had counted seven hours and seven minutes, King Midas opened the car door and got in, but immediately found himself sitting in a great big pile of manure, because it was still seven minutes until the spell wore off.

THE BLUE
STOPLIGHT

Once upon a time, the stoplight that stands in Piazza del Duomo in Milan did something very peculiar. Suddenly, all its lights turned blue, and people no longer knew what to do.

"Should we cross or shouldn't we? Should we stop or should we go?"

From all its eyes, in all directions, the stoplight sent out an unusual signal: a blue light that was so blue, the skies over Milan had never been so blue.

While waiting to figure out what was happening, the motorists shouted and honked their horns, the motorcyclists made their engines roar, and the bossiest pedestrians said loudly, "My good man, you have no idea who I am!"

Witty wags tossed out observations: "The fat cat must have gobbled up all the green to build himself a nice little villa in the countryside."

"Maybe they used the red to dye the municipal fire engines."

"You know what they used the yellow for? They added it to the olive oil to earn more money per bottle."

At last, a traffic cop arrived and took up a position at the center of the intersection, where he began directing traffic. Another cop pulled open the control box to try to fix the problem, and he turned off the electricity.

But just before the power was cut, the blue stoplight had enough time to think: *Poor fools! I was giving them the go ahead for the sky. If they'd only understood me, now they would all know how to fly. Maybe they were just too scared.*

112

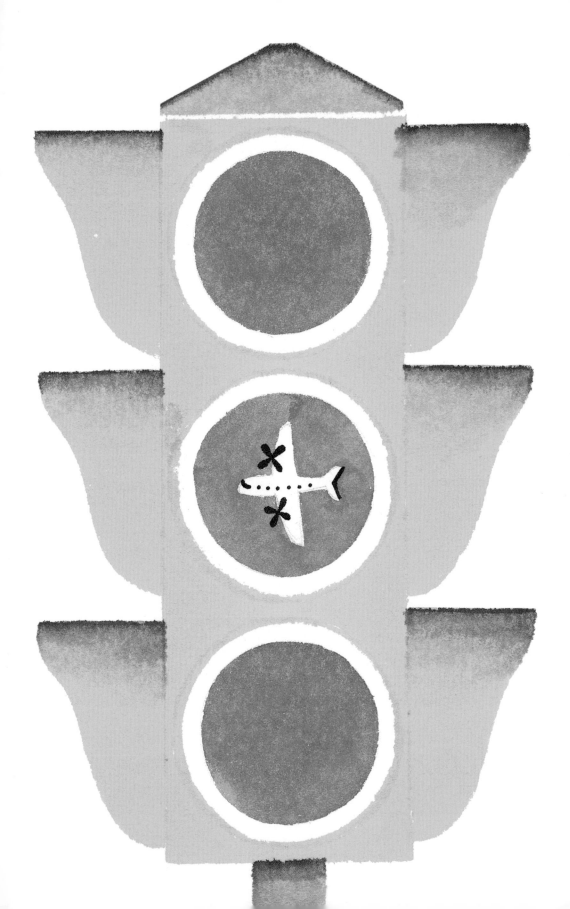

BRING DOWN THE NINE

A pupil was doing long division. "Three goes into thirteen four times, with a remainder of one. That means the quotient is four. Three times four is twelve, twelve from thirteen is one. Bring down the nine ..."

"Oh, no you don't!" shouted the nine.

"I beg your pardon?" asked the pupil.

"Why do you have it in for me? Why did you cry, 'Bring down the nine'? What did I ever do to you? Do you think of me as a public enemy?"

"But I was just—"

"Ah, I'm not surprised at all. I expected all along that you'd have an excuse in your back pocket. But that doesn't go down easy with me. You can cry, 'Bring down the house,' or, 'Bring down the sheriff,' and maybe even, 'Bring down the hot air.' But why would you ever want to say, 'Bring down the nine'?"

"Excuse me, but actually—"

"Don't interrupt. That's bad manners. I'm just a single-digit number, and any two-digit number can lord it over me all day long, but I still have a right to my numerical dignity! I demand respect. Especially from little snot-nosed kids like you. So bring down your luggage, bring down the price, but leave me out of it."

Confused and intimidated, the young student neglected to bring down the nine, got the wrong answer, and received a bad grade on his long division. Sad to say, sometimes you can just be too considerate.

TONINO THE INVISIBLE BOY

Once upon a time, a boy named Tonino went to school. He hadn't done his reading, and he was very worried that the schoolteacher might test him.

"Ah," he said to himself. "If only I could become invisible."

The teacher took the roll call, and when he got to Tonino's name, the boy replied, "Here!" But no one heard him, and the teacher said, "Too bad Tonino didn't come in today. I was planning to test him. If he's sick, let's just hope it's nothing serious."

And so Tonino realized that he had turned invisible, just as he'd wished. He jumped straight out of his chair for joy and wound up in the wastebasket. He got back on his feet and wandered around the classroom, pulling this or that boy's hair and overturning inkwells. Noisy arguments broke out, quarrel after quarrel. The pupils accused each other of having played those pranks, though none of them would ever have dreamed that the blame really belonged to Tonino the Invisible.

Once he tired of that game, Tonino left school and boarded a city bus—without paying the fare, of course, because the conductor couldn't see him. He found an empty seat and sat down. At the next stop, a lady with a large bag of groceries got on and started to sit down right where he had, because as far as she could see, it was still empty. But instead, she sat down next to him, putting her bag right on Tonino's lap, practically suffocating him, before she jumped up, shouting, "What kind of trick is this?! Can't a person even sit down anymore? Look here, I'm putting my bag of groceries down, and it just floats in midair."

116

What she couldn't see was that the bag was actually resting on Tonino's knees. A huge argument broke out, and nearly all the passengers launched into furious complaints against the bus company.

Tonino got off the bus in the center of town, slipped into a pastry shop, and started grabbing pastries to his heart's content: currant buns, chocolate beignets, and sweets of every type and description. The sales clerk, who noticed the pastries vanishing from the counter, blamed a dignified gentleman who was buying a bag of candy lifesavers for an elderly aunt.

The gentleman protested. "Are you calling me a thief? You, madame, don't know who you're talking to. You don't know who my father was. You don't know who my grandfather was!"

"And I don't want to know them, either," the sales clerk replied.

"How dare you insult my grandfather!"

A terrible quarrel ensued, and the police came running. But Tonino the Invisible slipped between the lieutenant's legs and headed back to school to watch his classmates being let out for the afternoon. And, in fact, he saw them being let out—or really, we should say he saw them pour down the school's front steps like an avalanche—but none of them caught so much as a glimpse of him. Tonino chased after this one or that, yanking his friend Roberto's hair, giving a lollipop to his friend Guiscardo. But they didn't see him and paid him no mind whatsoever, their gazes passing through him as if he were clear as glass.

Tired and a little disheartened, Tonino went home. His mother was on the balcony waiting for him.

"I'm home, Mama!" Tonino cried.

But she neither heard nor saw him and continued anxiously peering out at the street behind him.

"Here I am, Papa!" Tonino exclaimed once he was inside, sitting down at the table in his usual chair.

But his papa just murmured uneasily, "I wonder what could be keeping Tonino out so late? You don't think something terrible has happened to him, do you?"

117

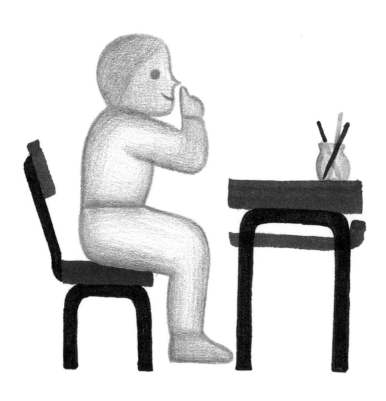

"But I'm here! I'm right here! Mama! Papa!" Tonino shouted. But they couldn't hear his voice.

By now, Tonino was in tears, but what good are tears, if no one can see them?

"I don't want to be invisible anymore," Tonino wailed, brokenhearted. "I want my father to see me, I want my mother to scold me, and I want my teacher to test me! I want to play with my friends! It's horrible to be invisible! It's awful to be all alone in the world."

He went out onto the staircase and walked slowly down to the courtyard.

"Why are you crying?" asked a little old man who was sitting on the bench and taking in the afternoon sun.

"What, can you see me?" asked Tonino anxiously.

"Of course I see you. I see you go to school and come back home every day."

"But I've never seen you, signore."

"Sure, I know that. No one ever notices me. An elderly retiree, all alone—why on earth would children look at me? For you, I'm just like the invisible man."

"Tonino!" his mama cried from the balcony just then.

"Mama, can you see me?"

"Ah, so you think I shouldn't see you, I suppose? Come upstairs right now and wait till your father gets a look at you."

"Coming right away, Mama!" Tonino shouted joyfully.

"Aren't you afraid of getting a spanking?" laughed the little old man.

Tonino threw his arms around the little old man's neck and gave him a kiss on the cheek.

"Thank you, sir, you've saved my life!" he cried.

"Oh, let's not exaggerate," said the little old man.

SO MANY
QUESTIONS

Once upon a time, there was a little boy who asked many, many questions. This wasn't a problem. In fact, it was a good thing. But it was very hard to find answers to the questions that the little boy liked to ask.

For instance, he would ask, "Why do drawers have tables?"

People would look at him, or they might answer, "Drawers are there to hold utensils."

"I know what drawers are for, but I don't know why drawers have tables."

People would shake their heads and walk away.

Another time, he asked, "Why do fins have fishes?" Or else, "Why do whiskers have cats?" In response to which, people would shake their heads and go about their business.

As the boy grew up, he never stopped asking questions.

And when he was a full-grown man, he still went around asking this, that, and the other. Since no one ever answered his questions, he withdrew to a cottage on a mountaintop and spent his time thinking of questions and writing them down in a notebook. Then he'd ponder and muse in search of answers, but he never found even one.

For instance, he would write, "Why does the shadow have a pine tree?"

"Why don't clouds write letters?"

"Why don't stamps drink beer?"

After writing down so many questions, he got a headache, but he paid no attention to it. His whiskers grew into a beard, but he didn't stop to shave. In fact, he just asked himself,

120

"Why do beards have faces?"

In short, he was quite a phenomenon. When he died, a scholar researched his life and discovered that ever since he was a small boy, he'd always put his socks on inside out, and he'd never once managed to get them on the right way. As a result, he had never learned to ask questions quite the right way. The same thing has happened to lots of other people.

GILBERTO
THE GOOD BOY

A good boy named Gilberto was very eager to learn, and so he always paid close attention to what grown-ups had to say.

One time, he heard a woman say, "Look at how Filomena loves her mother—she'd carry water for her with her ears."

Good little Gilberto thought to himself, *What magnificent words. I'm going to learn them by heart!*

A short while later, his mama asked him, "Gilberto, would you go and get me a pail of water from the fountain?"

"Right away, Mama," said Gilberto. But as he replied, he was thinking, *I want to prove to Mama how much I love her. Instead of using the pail, I'll carry the water back to her in my ears.*

He went to the fountain, put his head under the running water, and filled one of his ears. However, it held only a thimbleful of water, and in order to carry that water home, good little Gilberto had to hold his head twisted to one side.

"Is that water ever coming?" grumbled his mother, since she needed the water to wash the linen.

"Coming, Mama," Gilberto replied, hurrying even faster. But in order to answer her, he had to straighten his head, and the water poured out of his ear and ran down his neck. He ran back to the fountain to fill the other ear. It held the exact same amount of water as the first ear, and good little Gilberto had to keep his head tilted to one side, so before he got home, all the water had dribbled out.

"Is the water coming?" his mother asked again, irritation in her voice.

Maybe my ears are just too small, good little Gilberto thought sadly.

In the meantime, his mother had run out of patience. She assumed that Gilberto had been fooling around at the fountain, and so when she saw him, she reached out and boxed him on both ears.

Poor little, good little Gilberto.

He took the boxing and said nothing, having decided that next time, he'd carry the water in a pail.

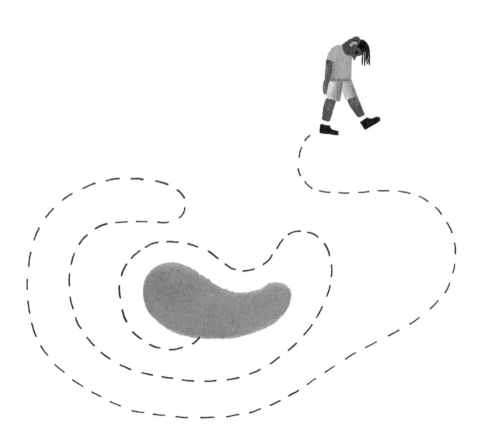

THE WORDS:
TO CRY

This story hasn't happened yet, but it will surely happen tomorrow. Here is what it says.

Tomorrow, a kind old schoolmistress will lead her pupils in a line, two by two, on a tour of the Museum of Bygone Times, which houses a vast collection of things that are no longer used, such as a king's crown, a queen's long silk train, the tram to Monza, and so on.

In a somewhat dusty display case are the words "To cry."

The young pupils of tomorrow will read the sign, but they won't understand it.

"Teacher, what does that mean?"

"Is it an antique jewel?"

"Did it once belong to the Etruscans, perhaps?"

The teacher will explain that once upon a time, that word was widely used, and it was very sorrowful. She will show them a vial that contains old tears. Who knows? Perhaps a person beaten up by another had shed them, or a homeless child had wept them.

"It looks like water," says one of the pupils.

"But it scalded and burned," says the teacher.

"Did they boil it before using?"

The young pupils simply couldn't understand. In fact, they were already starting to get bored. And so, the good school teacher took them to visit other sections of the museum, where there were easier things to see, such as prison bars, a watchdog, the tram to Monza, and so on, all things that in the happy land of tomorrow will no longer exist.

GOBBLEDY FEVER

When a little girl gets sick, her dolls also need to get sick, to keep her company. Her grandfather comes to check up on her, prescribes the appropriate medicines, and gives her plenty of injections with a ballpoint pen.

"This little girl is sick, Doctor."

"Let's take a look. Oh yes, quite right. It seems to me she has a full-blown case of bronchiolitis."

"Is that serious?"

"Extremely serious. Give her some blue-pencil syrup and a therapeutic massage with a licorice candy wrapper."

"What about this other little girl? Doesn't she look a little ill to you, too, Doctor?"

"Deathly ill. You can see it even without a telescope."

"What does she have?"

"A wee bit of a common cold, a wee bit of an uncommon cold, and six ounces of acute strawberryitis."

"Oh, dear me! Is she going to die?"

"There's no danger of that. Just give her these stupidina tablets dissolved in a glass of dirty water, but make sure you use a green glass, because a red glass would be sure to give her a toothache."

One morning, the little girl wakes up all better. The doctor says she can get out of bed, but first her grandfather needs to approve. Cupping his hands, he says, "Let's have a listen. Say thirty-three; say parapeps; try singing a song. All is well! A magnificent case of gobbledy fever, if ever there was one."

126

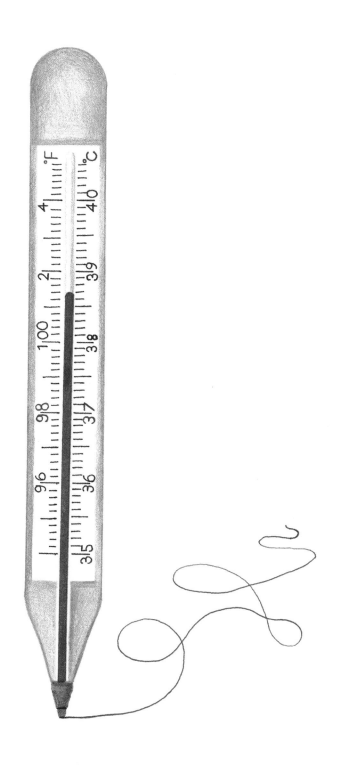

SUNDAY MORNING

Signor Cesare was a creature of habit. Every Sunday morning, he got up late, wandered around the house in his pajamas, and at eleven o'clock he would shave, leaving the bathroom door open.

That was the moment that Francesco was waiting for. He was only six, but he already showed a great deal of aptitude for medicine and surgery. Francesco got out the bag of cotton balls, the bottle of rubbing alcohol, and the box of bandages, and he went into the bathroom and sat down on the stool to wait.

"What is it?" asked Signor Cesare, as he lathered his face.

The other days of the week, he used an electric razor to shave, but on Sundays he still used shaving soap and razor blades, just like in the old days.

"What is it?"

Francesco was twisting on the little stool, as serious as could be, saying nothing in reply.

"Well?"

"Um," said Francesco, "you might be about to cut yourself. I'm here to help you."

"Right," said Signor Cesare.

"But don't cut yourself on purpose like you did last Sunday," Francesco said sternly. "Otherwise, it doesn't count."

"Of course not," said Signor Cesare.

But cutting himself without doing it on purpose was harder to do than you might think. He tried to make a mistake without meaning to, but that's difficult, almost impossible. He did everything he could to be careless, but he just couldn't get the blood to flow. Finally, though, there were tiny cuts here and there, and Francesco could finally spring into action. He dabbed a drop of blood with a cotton ball, disinfected the spot with the alcohol, and applied a bandage.

And so, every Sunday, Signor Cesare gave the gift of a drop of blood to his son, and Francesco became increasingly certain that he had a careless father.

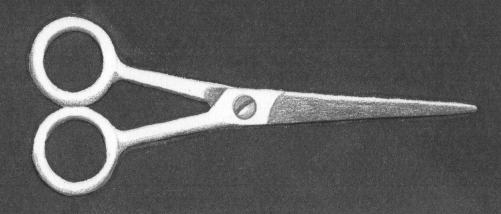

99%
Alcohol

SLEEPING, WAKING UP

Once upon a time, there was a girl who became little Teeny-Tiny every night, just as she was going to bed. "Mama," she would say, "I'm now an ant."

And her mother would know that it was time to put her to bed.

At sunrise, when the girl woke up, she would still be little Teeny-Tiny. So, when she stretched out on the pillow, there would still be plenty of pillow left.

"Time to get up," her mother would say.

"I can't," the little girl would reply. "I can't—I'm still too small. Now I'm like a butterfly. Wait for me to get big again."

After a while, she would squeal, "There! Now I'm big again."

And with a shout, she'd jump out of bed, and begin her new day.

GIACOMO
OF CRYSTAL

Once upon a time, in a faraway city, a transparent child came into the world. You could see through his limbs as if looking through air or water. He was made of flesh and bones, but also seemed to be made of glass, yet if he fell, he wouldn't shatter. At the very worst, he might get a transparent bump on his forehead.

You could see his heart beating, and you could see his thoughts twist and flash like colorful fish in their tank.

Once, by mistake, the child told a lie, and right away, everyone could see what seemed like a ball of flame behind his forehead. When he told the truth, the ball of flame dissolved. For the rest of his life, he never again told a lie.

Another time, a friend told him a secret, and immediately, everyone saw a sort of black ball spinning restlessly in his chest, and the secret was no longer a secret.

The child grew, became a young man, and then a full-grown man. Everyone could read his thoughts, and if they asked him a question, they could guess his response even before he opened his mouth.

His name was Giacomo, but people called him Giacomo of Crystal, and they loved him for his forthrightness and honesty.

Whoever was around him became kinder.

Unfortunately, in that land, a ferocious dictator seized power, and a period of bullying, abuses of power, injustice, and misery for the people began. Anyone who dared to protest promptly vanished without a trace.

Anyone who rose up in rebellion was executed by firing squad. The poor were persecuted, humiliated, and insulted in any of a hundred ways.

The people remained silent and submitted, fearful of the consequences.

But Giacomo didn't know how to remain silent. Even if he kept his mouth shut, his thoughts spoke for him. Because he was transparent, everyone could see his thoughts of indignation and condemnation for the tyrant's injustices and abuses. Over time, in secret, people started repeating Giacomo's thoughts and taking hope from them.

The tyrant ordered Giacomo of Crystal arrested and had him thrown into the gloomiest prison in the realm.

But then something incredible happened: The walls of the cell where Giacomo was locked up became transparent, and after that, so did the walls of the prison itself, as did the outer walls of the prison compound. People who passed by the prison could see Giacomo sitting on his stool, as if the prison itself were made of glass, and they continued to read his thoughts. At night, the prison cast a bright light, and the tyrant ordered all the curtains in his palace to be drawn, so he wouldn't have to see it.

Even so, he was unable to get to sleep. Despite his chains, Giacomo of Crystal was far more powerful than the tyrant, because the truth is stronger than anything else, more luminous than broad daylight, and more threatening to injustice than a hurricane.

MONKEYS ON HOLIDAY

One day, the monkeys in the zoo decided to go on an educational field trip. They walked and walked, and when they stopped, one of them asked, "What can you see?"

"The lion's cage, the seals' tank, and the giraffe's house."

"What a big world we live in, and how informative it is to travel."

They started walking again, and they didn't stop until it was noon.

"What can you see now?"

"The giraffe's house, the seals' tank, and the lion's cage."

"What a strange world we live in, and how educational it is to travel."

They started walking again, and they didn't stop until the sun had set.

"What can you see now?"

"The lion's cage, the seals' tank, and the giraffe's house."

"What a boring world we live in, with always the same things to see. And traveling doesn't do a bit of good."

Of course not. They had been traveling and traveling, but without ever having left their cage. All they had been doing was going around and around in circles, like the horses on a merry-go-round.

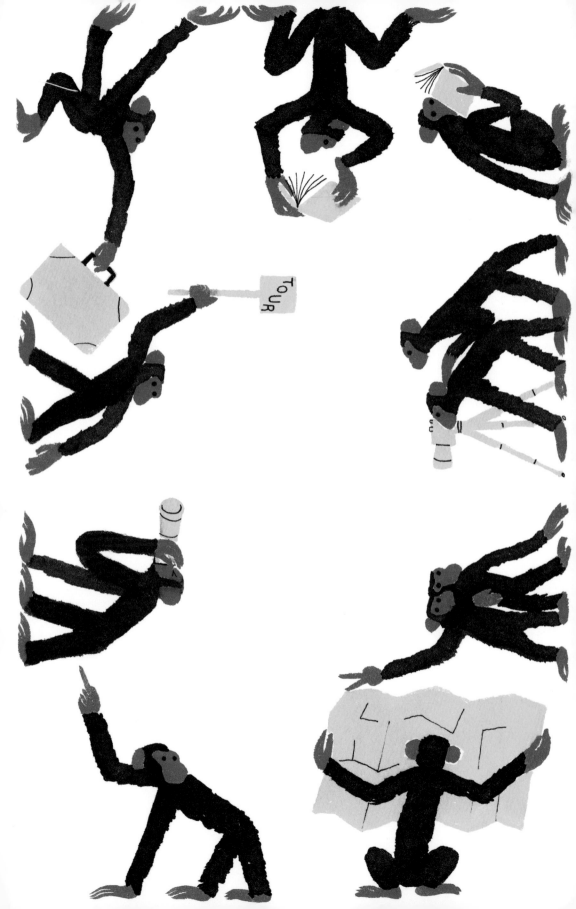

SIGNOR FALLANINNA

Signor Fallaninna was very delicate. So delicate that if a millipede walked on the wall, he couldn't sleep because of the noise; and if an ant dropped a grain of sugar, he'd jump to his feet and shout in terror, "Help! Help! An earthquake!"

Naturally, he couldn't stand little children, thunderstorms, or motorcycles, but more than anything else, what annoyed him was having dust under his feet, and so he never walked anywhere, not even indoors. Instead, he had himself carried everywhere by his servant, who was very strong. This servant's name was Guglielmo, and from daybreak to nightfall, Signor Fallaninna never stopped shouting at him and upbraiding him. "Gently, Guglielmo! Nice and gently. Otherwise, you'll break me."

Since he never walked anywhere, he got fatter and fatter, and the fatter he got, the more delicate he became. Even the calluses on Guglielmo's hands were starting to bother him.

"Guglielmo, how many times do I have to tell you that you need to put on your gloves when you carry me?"

Guglielmo heaved a sigh and laboriously put on a pair of oversized gloves that would have been too big for a hippopotamus.

But Signor Fallaninna just got heavier with every passing day, and poor Guglielmo sweated in the winter as if it were summer, and one fine day, it occurred to him: What would happen if I threw Signor Fallaninna off the balcony?

It just so happened that on that very day, Signor Fallaninna had put on a white linen suit, and when Guglielmo threw him off the balcony, Signor Fallaninna happened to land on a speck of fly poop and got a stain on his clean white trousers.

You'd need a magnifying glass to even see it, but Signor Fallaninna was so delicate that he died of mortification.

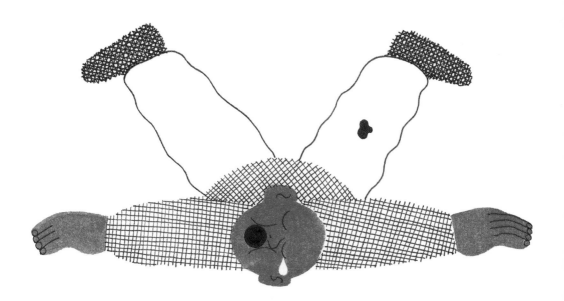

ONE AND SEVEN

I met a boy who was seven boys.

He lived in Rome, his name was Paolo, and his father was a trolley conductor.

But he also lived in Paris, where his name was Jean, and his father worked in a car factory.

He also lived in Berlin, and there, his name was Kurt, and his father gave him cello lessons.

But he also lived in Moscow, where his name was Yuri, just like the cosmonaut Gagarin, and his father was a bricklayer, who also studied math.

And he lived in New York, where his name was Jimmy, and his father owned a gas station.

How many have I said so far? Five.

There are two left over. One's name was Chu, he lived in Shanghai, and his father was a fisherman. The last one's name was Pablo, he lived in Buenos Aires, and his father was a house painter.

Paolo, Jean, Kurt, Yuri, Jimmy, Chu, and Pablo were seven little boys, but they were also the same little boy, eight years old, who already knew how to read and write and ride a bike with no hands. Paolo had black hair, Jean was blond, and Kurt had brown hair, but they were all the same little boy. Yuri had pale skin, and Chu had olive skin, but they were the same little boy. Pablo went to Spanish movies, and Jimmy went to movies in English, but they were still the same little boy, and they laughed in the same language.

Now all seven of those boys have grown up, but they will never be able to wage war on each other, because all seven of them are one and the same man.

THE MAN WHO STOLE THE COLOSSEUM

Once upon a time, a man got it into his head to steal the Colosseum in Rome. He wanted to have it all to himself, because he didn't like having to share it with others. He got a bag and waited until the guard at the Colosseum was looking in the opposite direction. Then he hastily filled his bag with old stones and carried it home. The next day, he did the same thing, and every morning except for Sunday, he made at least a couple of trips, or even three, always taking great care that the guards did not catch him. On Sunday, he rested and counted the stolen stones, which were piling up in his basement.

When his cellar was full, he started piling the stones up in the attic, and when the attic was full, he concealed them underneath the sofas, in the cupboards, and in the laundry hamper. Every time he went back to the Colosseum, he observed carefully in all directions and thought to himself how it might look largely the same, but it was still possible to detect a certain difference, like in that one area where it was already a little smaller. And wiping the sweat from his brow, he would scratch away at a piece of brick until he had pried it loose from a tier of seats, or detached a small stone from the arches, and filled up his bag.

Ecstatic tourists strode past him time and again, open-mouthed in astonishment, and he would laugh with gusto, although he covered his mouth. *Ah, how your jaws will drop the day you no longer see the Colosseum!*

If he went to the tobacconist, the color postcards with views of the magnificent amphitheater delighted him. He had to get out his handkerchief and pretend he was blowing his nose, so no one would see him laughing. Hee, hee, hee! Color postcards. Soon enough, if they want to see the Colosseum, they'll have to buy a postcard and settle for that.

Months turned into years. By that time, the stolen stones were heaped under his bed. They also filled the kitchen, leaving room only for a narrow passageway between the gas stove and the sink. They were also piled high in the bathtub, and had transformed the hallway into a stone quarry. But the Colosseum was still in its place—not a single arch was missing. Even a mosquito working to demolish it with its tiny forepaws wouldn't have left it so wholly intact.

The poor thief, as he aged, was swept up in a surge of despair. He thought, *Could I have gotten my calculations wrong? Maybe it would have been smarter to steal the dome of St. Peter's Cathedral? But come, come. Buck up! When you make a decision, you need to stick with it to the bitter end.*

At this point, every trip cost him greater and greater effort and pain. The bag cut into his arms and made his hands bleed. When he felt that he was on the verge of death, he dragged himself one last time all the way to the Colosseum and struggled his way up, tier by tier, until he reached the highest terrace. The setting sun tinged the ancient ruins with shades of gold, purple, and violet, but the poor old man couldn't see anything, because his tears and exhaustion blurred his vision. He had hoped he would be up there alone, but already tourists were crowding onto the little terrace, crying out in astonishment in all their various languages. And there, amid all those different voices, the elderly thief discerned the silvery notes of a child's voice, as he cried, "It's mine! It's mine!"

How it clashed! How out of place the word "mine" seemed all the way up there, overlooking such beauty. The old man finally understood it, and he wished that he could explain it to the little boy. He wanted to teach him to say "ours" instead of "mine," but he lacked the strength to do so.

ELEVATOR
TO THE STARS

At the age of thirteen, Romoletto was hired as assistant delivery boy at the Bar Italia. He was put in charge of home deliveries, and all day long, he ran up and down streets and stairways, balancing trays piled dangerously high with shot glasses, demitasses, and cocktail glasses. What bothered him most were the stairs. In Rome—like everywhere else on Earth, for that matter—the doormen are jealous of their elevators, and they forbid access, either in person or else with signs, to bar delivery boys, milkmen, fruit vendors, and the like.

One morning, a call came in from apartment number 14 at street number 103. The order was for four beers and one iced tea: "But right away! Otherwise, I'll throw them all out the window," added an ill-tempered voice—the voice of the elderly Marchese Venanzio, the terror of all local tradesmen.

The elevator at number 103 was one of those that was strictly off-limits to tradesmen, but Romoletto knew how to get around the menacing doorman, who was catnapping in his booth. He scampered unseen into the elevator car, slipped the required five-lire coin into the slot, pushed the button for the sixth floor, and the elevator started up with a creak. Here was the second floor, the third, then the fourth. After the fifth floor, however, instead of slowing down, the elevator suddenly sped up and shot past Marchese Venanzio's landing without stopping.

Before Romoletto had time to be astonished, all of Rome lay spread out beneath him, and the elevator was rocketing upward into a sky so blue that it seemed black.

144

"So long, Marchese Venanzio," Romoletto murmured with a shiver. With his left hand, he was still carefully balancing the tray with the drinks. It seemed almost funny, since the elevator was surrounded by increasingly vast expanses of interplanetary space, while the Earth, far below, was spinning on its axis, dragging Marchese Venanzio along in its orbit, as he waited for the four beers and the iced tea.

At least I won't arrive among the Martians empty-handed, Romoletto thought, as he closed his eyes. When he opened them, the elevator had started to descend again, and Romoletto heaved a sigh of relief that the tea would get there still iced, after all.

Unfortunately, the elevator landed in the heart of a wild tropical rain forest, and Romoletto, gazing out through the glass, saw himself surrounded by strange bearded creatures that pointed at him in excitement, chattering away at extraordinary speed in an incomprehensible language. *Perhaps we've fallen to Earth in a most out-of-the-way place*, thought Romoletto. But behold! The circle of creatures parted to make way for an unexpected personage: a humongous creature in a dark-blue uniform, sitting on an enormous tricycle.

A police officer! Time to get going, Romoletto!

And without waiting to count to one or even two, the young delivery boy of the Bar Italia pushed one of the elevator's buttons, the first one his finger chanced to touch. The elevator took off at supersonic speed, and only when it had traveled a considerable distance did Romoletto realize, as he looked down, that the planet he was escaping could not possibly be Earth. Its continents and its oceans had a completely different design, and while Earth as seen from space had struck him as being a tender light blue, the colors of this globe varied from green to purple.

It must have been Venus, Romoletto decided, *but how am I going to explain this to Marchese Venanzio?*

He touched the knuckles of his hand to the glasses on the tray. They were as ice-cold as when he'd left the bar. All things considered, it couldn't have been more than a few minutes.

145

The elevator, after rocketing though an enormous expanse of empty space at incredible velocity, began to descend again. This time, Romoletto could have no doubts. "Goodness gracious!" he exclaimed. "We're landing on the moon. What am I doing here?"

The famous lunar craters were rapidly coming closer.

Romoletto darted the fingers of his free hand away from the tray to the buttons on the elevator, and he was about to push one when he commanded himself to "Hold on!" before randomly pushing just any old button. "Let's give this a little thought," he said to himself.

He studied the row of buttons. The bottom button had a red letter "G," which stood for "ground."

"Let's give that a try," sighed Romoletto, who was eager to get his feet back on solid ground.

He pushed the button for the ground floor, and the elevator immediately reversed direction. A few minutes later, it was crossing the sky over Rome again, then it plunged through the roof of number 103, down the stairwell, landing on the ground floor, right next to the familiar doorman's booth, where the doorman, blissfully oblivious to that interplanetary drama, continued to slumber.

Romoletto hurried out of the elevator cabin without even bothering to turn around and close the doors behind him. This time, he went upstairs on foot. He knocked at the door of apartment 14 and listened, head down, silent, to the scolding he got from Marchese Venanzio. "Well, where have you been all this time? Do you know that it's been no less than fourteen minutes since I ordered these darned beers and this double-darned iced tea? If it had been Yuri Gagarin instead of you, he would already have landed on the moon."

Even further, thought Romoletto, but he didn't utter a word. And luckily, the drinks were still perfectly ice cold.

Yes, on any given workday, the delivery boy for the Bar Italia has to travel quite some distance …

146

BUS NUMBER 75

One morning, instead of turning down toward Trastevere from Monteverde Vecchio for Piazza Fiume, bus number 75 roared up the Gianicolo Hill, turned off down the Via Aurelia Antica, and in a matter of minutes was racing through the meadows outside of Rome like a wild rabbit on vacation.

The passengers at that time of the morning were almost all office workers with jobs to get to, and they were reading the morning paper—even the ones who hadn't bought a paper, because they were reading over their neighbors' shoulder. One man, as he was turning the page, happened to look up for a moment, and what he saw out the window made him start. "Conductor!" he shouted. "What on earth is happening? Treason, betrayal!"

All the other passengers looked up from their papers, as well, and soon their cries of protest swelled into a blustery chorus.

"Hey, this is the way to Civitavecchia!"

"What's gotten into the driver's head?"

"He's lost his mind. Tie him up!"

"What the heck kind of service is this!"

"It's ten minutes to nine, and at ten o'clock on the dot, I have to be in court!" shouted a lawyer. "If I lose this case, I'll bring a lawsuit against the bus company."

The conductor and the driver did their best to fend off the attack, declaring that they knew no more about what was happening than any of the passengers and that the bus had simply stopped responding to the controls and was now doing

148

just as it pleased. And indeed, at that very moment, the bus veered off the road and came to a halt at the edge of a cool, sweet-smelling grove of trees.

"Oooh, cyclamens!" exclaimed a woman in a burst of joy.

"I hardly think this is the time to be thinking about cyclamens," retorted the lawyer.

"What does it matter?" she replied. "I'll be late to work at the ministry, and my boss will yell at me, but what does that matter? As long as I'm here, I want to enjoy myself and pick some cyclamens. It must have been ten years since I picked one. "

She got off the bus, filling her lungs with fresh air on that peculiar morning, and started plucking a bouquet of cyclamens.

Seeing that the bus gave no signs of wishing to budge, the passengers got off one after the other to stretch their legs, and as they did, their bad moods evaporated like fog in bright sunlight. One man picked a daisy and put it in his buttonhole; another found a wild strawberry and shouted, "I discovered it, and it's mine! I'm going to put my business card down right here, and once it's ripe, I'm coming back to pick it, and you'll all be in trouble if I don't find it."

Suiting action to words, he pulled one of his business cards out of his wallet, drove a toothpick through it, and stuck the toothpick in the ground right next to the wild strawberry. Written on the card were these words: "Doctor Giulio Bollati."

Two employees of the Ministry of Education crumpled up their newspapers and started a game of soccer. Every time they kicked the ball, they shouted, "To heck with it!"

In other words, they hardly seemed like the same office workers who just a moment earlier had been ready to attack the driver and conductor.

The two municipal bus employees, in the meantime, were splitting a frittata panino and enjoying a little picnic on the grass.

"Look out!" the lawyer shouted suddenly.

The bus, with a shudder, was starting up again all on its own, moving along at a gentle trot. They all barely managed

149

to hop back aboard in time, and the last one to get on was the woman with the cyclamens, who objected loudly, "Hey, now, that's no fair. I was starting to enjoy myself."

"What time is it?" someone asked.

"Oooh, I wonder how late it is."

And they all glanced at their wristwatches. But surprise, surprise! Their watches still said it was ten minutes to nine. Evidently, the whole time they'd been enjoying their little excursion into the countryside, the minute hand hadn't budged. They had been given the gift of time, a little bonus, like when you buy a box of laundry detergent and inside there's a toy.

"This just can't be!" cried the woman with the cyclamens, as the bus retraced its route and roared down Via Dandolo.

Everyone was astonished. And yet they had the day's newspaper right there under their noses, and at the top of the newspaper was the date for all to see: March 21.

On the first day of spring, anything can happen.

DOG TOWN

Once upon a time, there was a strange little town. It consisted of a total of ninety-nine little houses, and each little house
had a little yard with a little gate, and behind each gate was
a barking dog.

Let's take an example. Fido was the dog in house number one, and he jealously protected the people who lived in
it. In order to do that, he would bark conscientiously every
time he saw someone go by, be it an inhabitant of any of the
ninety-eight other houses—man, woman, or child. The other
ninety-eight dogs behaved in exactly the same way, so they
were constantly busy barking day and night because there
was always someone walking on the road.

Let's take another example. The gentleman who lived in
little house number ninety-nine was obliged to walk past
ninety-eight other houses on his way home from work, and
so past ninety-eight dogs, all of whom barked at him, baring
their fangs, clearly, willing to sink their teeth into the seat of
his pants. The same went for the inhabitants of the other little
houses, and so there was always someone frightened walking
down the road.

That was just for residents of the town, so you can imagine
if an outsider came around—then all ninety-nine dogs started
barking at the same time. The ninety-nine housewives all
went out to see what was happening, and then hurried back
inside, bolted their doors shut, hastily lowered their wooden
roller shutters, and hunkered down, silent as could be, behind
their windows, peeping out until the outsider had gone by.

What with all the barking dogs, the inhabitants of that town had all become a little hard of hearing, and they didn't talk much amongst themselves. For that matter, they had never had much to say, nor much interest in talking.

Little by little, as they became more and more accustomed to silence and sulking, they even forgot how to talk. In the end, the inhabitants of the houses started barking just like their dogs. Maybe they even thought they were talking, but every time they opened their mouths, what you heard was a sort of "bow-wow" that just gave you goose bumps. And so, the dogs barked, the men and women barked, and the children barked as they played, until the ninety-nine little villas seemed to have turned into ninety-nine kennels.

Still, they were charming. The windows had bright, clean curtains, and there were even geraniums and succulent plants on the balconies.

One day, during one of his famous journeys, Giovannino Vagabond happened that way. The ninety-nine dogs greeted him with a concert that would have tested the nerves of a concrete block. He asked a woman for directions, and she simply barked back at him. He complimented a little boy, and all he got in return was a plaintive howl.

It's clear, Govannino decided. *It's an epidemic.*

He requested a meeting with the mayor and told him, "I have a surefire remedy. First, knock down all the fences and gates. After all, the gardens will grow just fine, even if they're not behind bars. Second, let all the dogs go hunting. They'll have more fun, and they'll become gentler and better tempered. Third, throw a nice dance party, and after the first polka, you'll all learn to talk again."

The mayor replied, "Bow-wow!"

"I understand," said Giovannino. "The worst patient is one who's convinced he's perfectly healthy."

With that, he set off to continue his travels.

At night, many dogs barking in unison in the distance can often be heard. Those might be actual dogs, but they might also be the inhabitants of that strange little town.

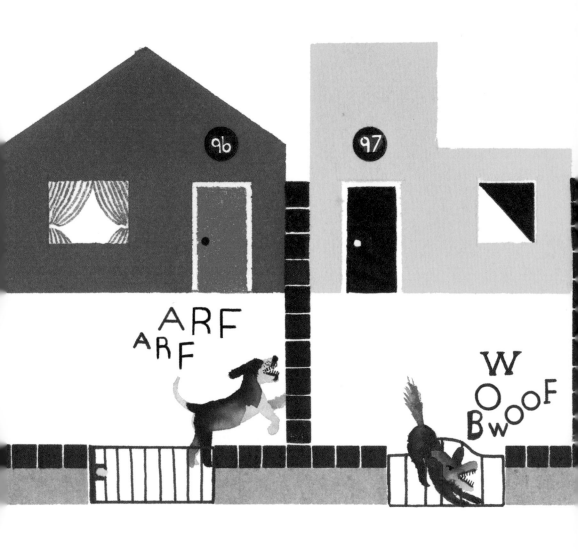

PULCINELLA'S ESCAPE

Pulcinella was the most restless marionette in the whole worn-and-tattered puppet theater. He always had one complaint or another, either because he preferred to go off on a stroll at the time the show was scheduled to begin, or because the puppeteer had assigned him a comical role, when he would much rather have had a dramatic part.

"One of these days," he confided to Harlequin, "I'm going to cut the strings that are tying me to this place." And he did, though it was one of these nights, not one of these days. In the darkness of the wee hours, he managed to get his hands on a pair of scissors that the puppeeer had left lying around, and he cut each of the strings that held up his head, hands, and feet. Then he whispered to Harlequin, "Come with me."

Harlequin, however, wasn't willing to be parted from Columbine, and Pulcinella had no intention of taking that smirking coquette along with him, especially considering the hundred-thousand tricks she'd played on him before audiences.

I'll just go alone, he decided. Courageously, he leapt down to the floor, and he was off, as fast as his legs could carry him.

How lovely, he thought, as he raced along, *not to feel all those strings tugging me in all directions. How lovely to set my foot exactly where I choose!*

The world is a vast and terrifying place to a solitary marionette, especially at night, when it is largely inhabited by ferocious cats eager to mistake anything that's fleeing for a mouse they can eagerly hunt. Pulcinella managed to talk the cats into believing that they were dealing with a genuine artist, but to make sure, he still took shelter in a secluded garden, where he squatted down against a low wall and fell fast asleep.

When the sun peeked over the horizon in the east, he woke up hungry. But all around him, as far as the eye could see, were nothing but carnations, tulips, zinnias, and hydrangeas.

"Oh well, I'll just have to make do," Pulcinella told himself. He picked a carnation and started chewing on its petals with cautious mistrust. It certainly was nothing like chewing on a grilled steak or a filleted fresh-caught perch. Flowers have a great deal of perfume but not much flavor. Still, to Pulcinella, that taste was the flavor of freedom, and by his second mouthful, he felt certain he'd never tasted a more delicious food in his life.

He decided that he would remain in that garden forever, and, in fact, he did. He slept in the shelter of a large magnolia whose tough leaves feared neither rain nor hail, and he fed himself on flowers. Today, a carnation; tomorrow, a rose. Pulcinella dreamed of mountains of spaghetti and prairies of mozzarella, but he refused to give in. He had become very thin, but was so sweet-smelling that sometimes bees would land on him, in hopes of finding nectar to drink. They'd buzz off in disappointment only after having tried in vain to sink their stingers into his wooden head.

Winter came, the garden withered in expectation of the first snows, and the poor marionette had nothing left to eat.

Don't say that he simply could have resumed his journey—his poor wooden legs wouldn't have carried him far.

"Oh, well," Pulcinella told himself, "I'll just die here. It's not a bad place to die. What's more, I'll die a free marionette. No one will ever again be able to tie a string to my head, to make me say yes or no."

The first snow buried him under a soft white blanket. When spring came, at that very spot, a carnation grew.

Calm and happy under the ground, Pulcinella was thinking, *Oh, look! A flower has grown over my head. Who could be happier than me?*

157

But Pulcinella wasn't dead, because a wooden marionette can never die. He's still there, under the ground, and no one knows it. If you're the one who happens to find him, never tie a string to his head. The kings and the queens of the puppet theaters don't mind it one bit, but Pulcinella simply can't take it.

THE BRICKLAYER
FROM VALTELLINA

A young man from Valtellina could find no work at home, so he emigrated to Germany, and it was in Berlin that he found a job on a construction site as a bricklayer. Mario—for that was the young man's name—was very pleased. He worked hard, ate very little, and every penny he earned, he set aside so he could be married.

But one day, while they were laying the foundations of a new apartment building, the scaffolding collapsed, and Mario fell into the wet, reinforced cement and died. It was impossible, however, to find his body deep in the foundation.

Mario was dead now, but he felt no pain. He was embedded in one of the columns of the building under construction, and he certainly had no room to move, but aside from that, he thought and felt more or less the same as before. Once he got used to his new situation, he was even able to open his eyes and admire the building as it rose around him. It really was as if he were supporting the weight of this new building, which made up for his sadness at not being able to send word home to his poor fiancée.

Hidden inside the wall, at its very heart, no one could see him or even suspected he was there, but that didn't matter to Mario.

The building rose all the way to the roof, doors and windows were installed, and the apartments were sold and purchased and filled with furniture. Last of all, many families came to live there. Mario got to know all the new inhabitants, from the eldest to the youngest. When babies toddled around

160

on the floors, practicing their first steps, they tickled his hands. When girls went out onto the balconies or leaned out the windows to watch their boyfriends pass by, Mario felt the softness of their locks brushing gently against his cheek.

In the evenings, he heard the dinner-table conversations of the families; at night, the hacking coughs of the sick; just before dawn, the jingling alarm clock of the baker, who was the earliest to rise. The life of the apartment building was Mario's life; the building's joys, floor by floor, and its sorrows, room by room, were his joys and his sorrows.

And then, one day, war broke out. Bombs were dropped all over the city, and Mario felt that the end was near for him as well. A bomb hit the apartment house and razed it to the ground. Nothing remained but a shapeless heap of rubble, shattered furniture, and crushed bric-a-brac, beneath which women and children who had been surprised in their sleep went on sleeping for all eternity.

It was only then that Mario really died—because the building that had come into this world through his sacrifice and had been a home to so many itself had died.

161

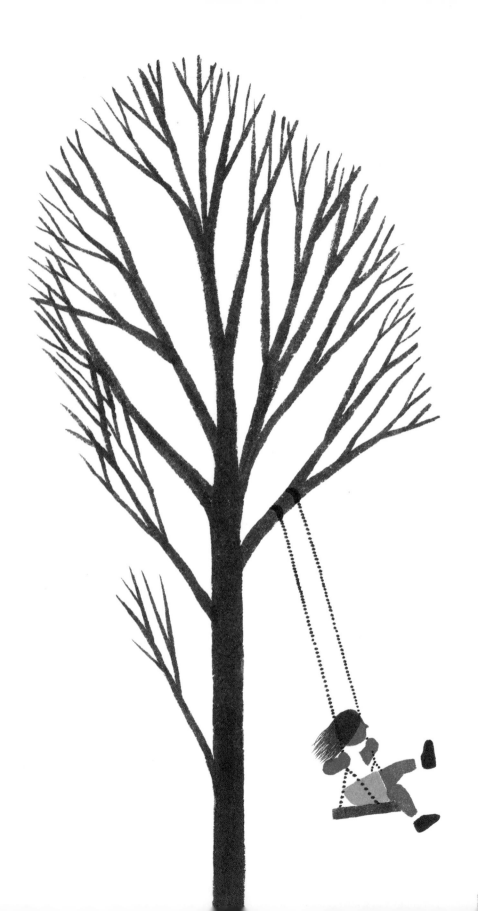

THE SOLDIER'S BLANKET

Private Vincenzo Di Giacomo, at the end of all the wars, came home with a tattered uniform, a bad cough, and a military blanket. The cough and the blanket represented all he'd earned in those long years of war.

"Now I'll get some rest," he told his family. But his cough wouldn't let him rest, and in a few months' time, it took him down into the grave.

His wife and children had nothing left to remember him by but the blanket. He had three sons, and the youngest of the three, born between one war and another, was just five years old. The soldier's blanket went to him. When he wrapped himself in it to sleep at night, his mother would tell him a long fairy tale, and in the fairy tale, there was always a fairy who was weaving a blanket big enough to cover all the children in the world and to keep them warm. There was always one child or another, however, who remained uncovered, and who cried and pleaded in vain for a hem of the blanket to warm him up. And so, the fairy had to undo all her work and start weaving a new blanket from scratch to make it a little bigger, because it had to be a single blanket, woven from start to finish, in a single piece—no additions could be patched on later. The good fairy worked day and night, weaving and unweaving, and she never tired. The little boy always fell fast asleep before the fairy tale had been fully told, and he never did find out how it all ended.

The littlest boy's name was Gennaro, and his small family lived in the area around Monte Cassino. The winter was very harsh. They had nothing to eat, and Gennaro's mother fell ill. Gennaro was given to neighbors who agreed to care for him. They were wanderers, with a wagon, and they traveled from town to town, making their living partly by begging, partly by playing the accordion, partly by selling the wicker baskets they wove on their stops along the road. They gave Gennaro a parrot in a cage that used its beak to pull a scrap of paper out of a box. On the pieces of paper were numbers to play in the lottery. It was Gennaro's job to show the parrot off to the people, and if they gave him a few coins, he'd let the parrot choose a number for them. The days were long and boring, and they often wound up in towns where the people were all poor and had nothing to give them in charity. When they went to towns and villages like that, Gennaro had to make do with a thinner slice of bread and an emptier bowl of soup. But when night fell, Gennaro would wrap himself in his soldier father's blanket, his one treasure, and in its sour warmth, he'd fall asleep, dreaming that a parrot was telling him a fairy tale.

One of the wanderers had served in the military with Gennaro's father. He became fond of the little boy, and he explained to Gennaro the hundreds of things they saw along the way. To stave off boredom, he taught Gennaro to read the signs with the names of the villages and cities.

"You see? That's an 'A.' That other skinny one that looks like a walking stick without a handle is an 'I.' That stick with a hunchback is a 'P.' "

Gennaro learned fast. The wanderer bought him a notebook and a pencil and taught him to copy the roadside signs. Gennaro filled pages and pages with the names of Ancona or Pesaro, and one day, he even managed to write his own name, with nobody's help, letter by letter without an error. What sweet dreams he had that night, wrapped in the blanket that had belonged to his father, the soldier.

And what a nice story this is, even if it never ends and just hangs there in midair, like a question mark without an answer.

G enova
E boli
N apoli
N izza
A ncona
R oma
O tranto

THE WELL
AT CASCINA PIANA

Midway between Saronno and Legnano, at the edge of a great forest, stood Cascina Piana, which all in all consisted of three large farmhouses with three communal courtyards. Eleven families lived there. In Cascina Piana, there was only a single well for drawing water, and it was a strange sort of well, because there was a pulley to wrap a rope around, but there was neither rope nor chain. Each of the eleven families kept a rope, as well as a bucket at home, and anyone who wanted to draw water from the well would take down the rope, sling it over their arm, and take it to the well. Once they had a pail of water, they took the rope off the pulley and purposefully took it back home, where they hung it up for safekeeping.

Only one well and eleven ropes. And if you don't believe me, just go and ask around for yourself, and they'll tell you—exactly as they told me—that those eleven families simply didn't get along and were constantly making mischief against each other. Rather than pooling their funds and buying a nice strong chain that they could fasten to the pulley for everyone to use, they would have sooner filled in the well with dirt and weeds.

But then war broke out, and the men of Cascina Piana went off to fight, but not before telling their women a great many things, including a strict admonition not to let anyone steal their well ropes.

Next, came the German invasion. The men were far away, and the women were afraid, but the eleven ropes stayed hidden away in the safety of the eleven different homes.

168

One day, a little boy from Cascina went to the woods to gather a bundle of firewood and heard a groan coming from behind a hedge. It was a partisan, wounded in the leg, and the little boy ran to fetch his mother. The woman was frightened, and she wrung her hands, but then she said, "We'll take him home and keep him hidden. Let's just hope that someone helps your father, who's fighting as a soldier now, if he ever needs it. We don't know where he is or even if he's still alive."

They hid the partisan in the grain loft and sent for the doctor, saying it was for the elderly grandmother. The other women of Cascina, however, had seen the grandmother that very morning, healthy as a young rooster, and they guessed that something fishy was afoot. Before twenty-four hours had passed, the whole town knew that there was a wounded partisan in that grain loft, and a few old farmers were starting to say, "If the Germans find out, they'll come here and kill us all. We'll all come to a bad end."

But that's not how the women thought about it. They thought about their men, far away, and they thought that they, too, might well be injured and trying to hide, and they heaved deep sighs. On the third day, one woman took a salami from the hog they'd just butchered and brought it to Caterina, the woman who had hidden the partisan, and told her, "That poor man needs to recover his strength. Give him this salami."

A short while later, another woman arrived with a bottle of wine, then a third with a bag of yellow corn meal to make polenta, then a fourth with a chunk of lard, and before evening fell, all the women of Cascina had been to visit Caterina, and they'd all seen the partisan, and they'd all brought their gifts, wiping away a tear as they did.

And the whole time that it took the wound to heal, all eleven families who lived at Cascina treated the partisan like a son, making sure he wanted for nothing.

When the partisan was healed, he went out into the courtyard to bask in the sun. He saw the well without a rope and was greatly astonished. The women blushed and explained to

him that every family had a rope of its own, but they couldn't provide him with a satisfactory explanation of that odd state of affairs. They were tempted to tell him that they were all enemies, but this was no longer strictly true, because they had all suffered together, and together, they had helped the partisan. So even though they hadn't realized it yet, they'd all become friends and sisters, and there was no longer any reason to keep eleven different ropes for the well.

They decided to pool their funds and buy a single chain for all the families and to hook it permanently to the pulley.

And so, they did. And the partisan drew the first bucket of water from the well, and it was something like the inauguration of a monument.

That same evening, the partisan, fully healed, set off again for the mountains.

HOUSES AND APARTMENT BUILDINGS

I went to the old people's home to visit with an elderly brick-layer. We hadn't seen each other in a great many years.

"Have you traveled?" he asks me.

"Well, I've been to Paris."

"Paris, eh? I've been there myself, many years ago. We were there to build a fine apartment building right on the banks of the river Seine. I wonder who lives there now? So, where else have you been?"

"I've been to America."

"America, eh? I've been there, too, many, many years ago. Who knows how long ago that was? I've been to New York, to Buenos Aires, Saõ Paulo, and Montevideo. Always building houses and apartment buildings and raising flags on the roofs. How about Australia? Have you been there?"

"No, not yet."

"Well, I've been there too. I was young back then. I wasn't a bricklayer yet; I carried pans full of mortar, and I sifted sand through the sieve. We were building a villa for a local gentleman, and a very nice gentleman at that. Once, as I re-call, he asked me how to cook spaghetti, and he wrote down everything I told him. What about Berlin? Have you been there?"

"Not yet."

"Eh, I went there before you were born. Beautiful build-ings we put up there—nice, strong houses. I wonder if they're still standing? Have you been to Algiers? What about Cairo, in Egypt?"

"I'm hoping to go this summer, in fact."

"Eh, you'll see handsome houses everywhere you look. Not to brag, but my walls have always gone up straight, and there's never been a leak in any of my roofs—not so much as a drop of water."

"You certainly have built a few houses in your time ..."

"Yep, one or two, not to brag, here and there around the world."

"And you—how are you?"

"Ack, what with me building all these houses for other people, I don't have a house of my own, as you can see. So, here I am in an old-age home. That's just how the world works."

Yes, that *is* how the world works, but it doesn't mean it's right.

MAESTRO GARRONE

Newfangled developments. Everywhere you look, there are newfangled developments.

Santa Claus arrived this year aboard a seventeen-stage rocket, and on every platform, there was a cabinet filled to bursting with presents, and in front of every cabinet, there was an electronic robot with the addresses of all the children. Not only all good children—all children. Because there's no such thing as a bad child, and at last, Santa Claus has learned this lesson.

Carnival saw newfangled developments too. Old Pulcinella put on a space suit, Gianduia tossed confetti out of a silver Sputnik, and the rococo damsels and the Blue Fairy hovered after the masquerade procession in a helicopter.

As did Easter. When we broke the chocolate egg, who leaped out? Surprise! A little yellow Martian chick with an antenna on his cap. Turns out the egg was a flying-saucer egg.

(Read the whole story of the little yellow cosmic chick on page 188)

Newfangled developments everywhere you look. So why is Maestro Garrone (the grandson of the estimable Garrone in the book *Heart*) so down in the mouth?

"My dear Signor Gianni," he says, "I like newfangled developments as well as anyone else. What wonderful machinery they have in the factories, what lovely spaceships in the sky. And refrigerators! What magnificent progress. But my school, have you seen it? It's exactly the same as it was back in the day of my grandfather Garrone and his classmates—the little stonemason Rabucco, De Rossi, and Franti, that little delinquent. In that school, there's not even the shadow of any wonderful machinery. Just the same scratched-up, uncomfortable desks and chairs as ever. I wish that my school were as nice as a brand-new television set or a shiny new automobile. But who will help me?"

paper

YELLOW MARTIAN CHICK
und inside chocolate egg

Today's

$ 1.50

SANTA ARRIVES!
Aboard a 17-stage Rocket

NO BAD CHILDREN FOUND

THE PLANET
OF TRUTH

The following page is copied down from a history textbook used in the schools of the planet Mun, and it is about a great scientist named Brun. (By the way, on that planet all the words end in un. So, for instance, no one says, "The world"; they say, "Thun worlun." And "bowl of spaghetti" is "bowun oun spaghettun," and so on.) Here's what it says about Brun ...

"Brun, an inventor, who lived for two thousand years, is currently preserved in a refrigerator from which he'll re-awaken in forty-nine thousand centuries to resume his life. He was still a baby in swaddling clothes when he invented a machine for making rainbows, which operated on dish soap and water, but instead of just making soap bubbles, it produced rainbows of all shapes and sizes. You could extend these rainbows from one end of the sky to the other, and they served many purposes, such as clotheslines for hanging out laundry to dry, for instance. In nursery school, playing with a couple of wooden rods, he invented a drill for making holes in the water. The invention was much appreciated by fish-ermen, who used it to pass the time when the fish weren't biting.

"In elementary school, while still in first grade, he invent-ed a machine for tickling pears, a pot for frying ice, a scale for weighing clouds, a telephone for talking to rocks, a musical hammer, which played beautiful symphonies while driving nails, and so forth.

"It would take too long to list all his inventions. Let's just mention the most famous of them: the machine for telling

176

lies, which worked when you inserted tokens. For one token, you could hear fourteen thousand lies. The machine contained all the lies in the world—the lies that had already been told, the lies that people were thinking of at that very moment, and all the others that would be invented in the future. Once the machine had recited all the possible lies, people were forced to always tell the truth. That's why the planet Mun is also known as the Planet of Truth.

THE CONVEYOR SIDEWALK

On planet Beh, they've invented a moving sidewalk that runs all around the city. It's like an escalator, but instead of stairs, it's a sidewalk, and it moves slowly, to give people time to look at shop windows and to get on or off without losing their balance. There are even benches on the sidewalk for people who want to travel sitting down, especially old people or women carrying their groceries. When little old men grow tired of sitting in the park and staring at the same old tree, they often go for a ride on the sidewalks. They sit there, content and happy. Some read newspapers, others smoke cigars, and they all relax comfortably.

Thanks to the invention of this sidewalk, trolley cars, electric buses, and cars have been abolished. There are still streets, but they're empty of vehicles, and children use them to play ball. If a policeman even tries to confiscate the ball, then he has to pay a fine.

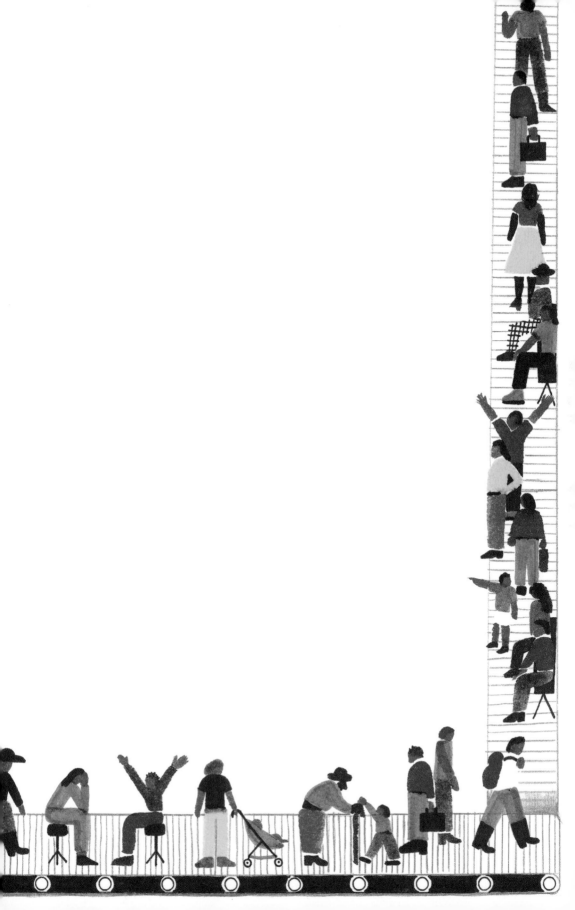

SPACE COOKING

A Russian astronaut friend of mine was on planet X213 recently and brought me back a souvenir: a menu from a space restaurant. I'll copy it all down for you, exactly as I see it:

APPETIZERS
River gravel in cork sauce
Blotter-paper bruschetta
Charcoal cold cuts

SOUPS AND PASTAS
Roses in broth
Carnation noodles with ink sauce
Roasted café-table legs
Pink marble fettuccine with a minced-lightbulb butter
Gnocchi with molten lead.

DISHES READY TO ORDER
Reinforced concrete chops
Grilled karate chops
Fried carrot chops and karate chips
Roast bricks with an asphalt-shingle salad
Turkey breastplates
Boiled car tires with piston croutons
Deep-fried water faucets (hot and cold)
Typewriter keys (in verse and in prose)

DISHES INDIVIDUALLY PREPARED
Upon request only.

In order to explain this last, somewhat generic expression, let me add that it would seem that planet X213 is entirely edible. There's nothing up there that you cannot eat and digest, even the asphalt on the streets.

What about the mountains? Those too. The inhabitants of X213 have already devoured entire alpine ranges.

Let's take a recent example. One of the planet's inhabitants goes for a bike ride in the country. He gets hungry, so he stops and eats the bike seat or the tire pump. Children are especially fond of bicycle bells.

A typical breakfast: The alarm clock goes off, you wake up, you grab the alarm clock, and you gobble it down in two bites.

EDUCATIONAL CANDY

On planet Bih, there are no books. Knowledge is sold in bottles, in drinkable form. History is a red liquid that resembles grenadine, geography is a minty green drink, and grammar is colorless and tastes like mineral water. There are no schools; kids study at home. Every morning, depending on their age, children have to gulp down a glassful of history, a few tablespoonsful of arithmetic, and so on.

But would you believe it? You still can't get them to do their lessons.

"Come on, now. Be a good boy," a mother says. "You just don't know how delicious zoology can be. It's sweet, sweet as sugar. Just ask Carolina." (Carolina is their electronic housekeeper robot).

Carolina very generously offers to taste the bottle's contents first. She pours a tiny dollop into a glass, drinks it, and smacks her lips. "Mm-mm! Very good!" she exclaims and immediately starts reeling off zoological facts: "A cow is a ruminant quadruped. It eats grass and gives us chocolate milk."

"You see?" the mother demands triumphantly.

The young pupil hangs back. He still suspects that it's not zoology at all, but cod-liver oil. At last he gives in, closes both eyes, and swallows the whole lesson in a single gulp. Applause.

It goes without saying that there are also diligent, hardworking young pupils. Indeed, some of them are gluttons for knowledge. They get up in the middle of the night to pilfer a little history grenadine, and they drain the glass to the very last delicious drop. They become prodigies of learning.

186

"Well, colonel is a higher rank than captain."

"Maybe where you live, because you have your ranks all backward. Where I come from, the highest rank is average citizen. But let's forget about that. My mission is a failure."

"We could tell you how sorry we are, but the truth is that we don't even know what your mission was."

"Ah, neither do I. All I know is that I was supposed to wait in that display counter until our secret agent got in touch with me."

"Interesting," said the professor. "So you all have secret agents here on Earth. What if we went and told the police all about it?"

"Be my guest. Go tell anyone you like about a cosmic chick—I'm sure they'll laugh right in your face."

"You're right about that. Well, since we're speaking privately, why don't you tell us something else about those secret agents?"

"They're assigned to identify the Earthlings who will land on Eighth Mars in twenty-five years."

"That's rather funny. We, for instance, don't even know where Eighth Mars is."

"Ah, but you forget, my dear professor, that up there we're twenty-five years ahead of you. For instance, we already know that the captain of the Earth spaceship that will land on Eighth Mars will be named Gino."

"Well, how do you like that," said Professor Tibolla's eldest son. "That's my name."

"Pure coincidence," decreed the cosmo chick. "His name will be Gino, and he will be thirty-three years old. Therefore, right now on Earth, he's exactly eight years old."

"Well, well, well," said Gino. "That's just how old I am."

"Would you stop interrupting me?!" the commander of the space egg sternly exclaimed. "As I was just explaining to you, we have to find this Gino and the other members of the future mission team so that we can keep an eye on them without their knowledge and in order to help bring them up properly."

189

THE COSMIC CHICK

Last Easter, at the home of Professor Tibolla, do you know what popped out of the chocolate Easter egg? Surprise! A cosmic chick, similar in every way to little yellow Earth chicks, but with a captain's cap on its head and a TV antenna perched atop the cap.

The professor, Signora Luisa, and the children all said, "Oh," in unison, and after that "Oh," they were speechless.

The chick looked around with a cross expression on its face.

"How behind the times you are on this planet," it observed. "Here, you're still having Easter; back home, on Eighth Mars, it's already Wednesday."

"Of this month?" asked Professor Tibolla.

"Of course not! Wednesday of next month. But in terms of years, we're twenty-five ahead of you."

The cosmic chick paced back and forth for a bit to stretch its legs, muttering as it paced, "How annoying! What an unfortunate annoyance."

"What are you worried about?" asked Signora Luisa.

"You broke my flying-saucer Easter egg, and now I won't be able to get back to Eighth Mars."

"But we bought the Easter egg at our local pastry shop."

"None of you know anything. This egg is actually a spaceship disguised as an Easter egg, and I'm the ship's commander, disguised as a little yellow chick."

"What about the crew?"

"Well, as it happens, I'm also the crew. But now I'm bound to be demoted. At the very least, they'll demote me to colonel."

HiSTORY

GEOGRAPHY

PHYSICS

Botany

ENGLiSH
GRAMMAR

GEOM ETRY

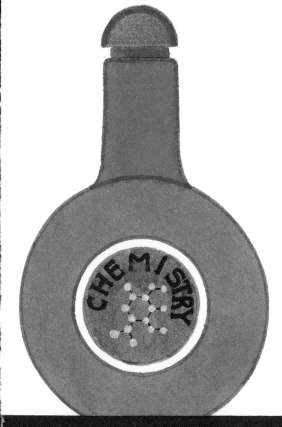

CHEMISTRY

ANATOMY

For children in nursery school, there are educational candies. They're strawberry, pineapple, and cordial flavored, and they contain a few simple poems, the names of the days of the week, and numbers up to ten.

A Russian astronaut friend of mine brought me one of those candies as a souvenir. I gave it to my little girl, and she immediately started reciting a funny rhyme in the language of planet Bih, which ran more or less like this: "Anta anta, pero pero, penta pinta pim però." And I didn't understand a word she said.

"What are you saying?" blurted out the professor. "Are you saying we aren't bringing our children up properly?"

"That's right. First of all, you aren't getting them used to the idea that they're going to have to engage in interstellar travel. Second, you failing to teach them that they're citizens of the universe. Third, you're not teaching them that the word 'enemy' is nonexistent outside of Earth. Fourth..."

"Excuse me, Commander," Signora Luisa interrupted him, "what's the last name of this Gino of yours?"

"I don't mind at all, but he's yours, not ours. He's called Tibolla. Gino Tibolla."

"But that's me!" cried the professor's son. "Hurrah!"

"What do you have to cheer about?!" exclaimed Signora Luisa. "Don't you think for one second that your father and I will allow you to ..."

But the cosmic chick had already flown straight into Gino's arms.

"Hurrah! Mission accomplished! In twenty-five years, I, too, will be able to return home."

"But what about the Easter egg?" asked Gino's little sister with a sigh.

"Why, we'll eat it, of course."

And so they did.

TELLING STORIES WRONG

"Once upon a time, there was a girl named Little Yellow Riding Hood!"

"You have it wrong, Grandpa! Little Red Riding Hood!"

"Oh, that's right! Little Red Riding Hood. Her mother called her one day and said, 'Listen, Little Green Riding Hood—'"

"No, Red!"

"Oh, that's right! Little Red Riding Hood. 'Now go to your Aunt Hildegard's house and take her this potato peel.'"

"No, 'Go to your grandma's house and take her this picnic basket full of goodies.'"

"Okay. So the little girl went into the deep, dark woods, and there, she met a giraffe."

"You're getting everything backward, Grandpa! She met a big bad wolf, not a giraffe."

"And the wolf asked her, 'How much is six times eight?'"

"No. Wrong. The wolf asked her, 'Where are you going?'"

"You're right. And Little Black Riding Hood answered—"

"It was Little Red Riding Hood! Red! Red!"

"Yes, and she answered, 'I'm going to the grocery store to buy some canned tomatoes.'"

"Not in your wildest dreams, Grandpa! It's 'I'm going to Grandmother's house, because she's sick, but I've lost my way.'"

"Right. So the horse said to her—"

"What horse? It was a wolf."

"Sure it was. And the wolf said, 'Here's what you do: Take

192

the number 75 bus, get off in front of the cathedral, take your first right, and you'll find three steps and a quarter lying on the sidewalk. Forget about the three steps, pick up the quarter, and go buy a packet of bubble gum.' "

"Grandpa, you really don't know how to tell a story. You get everything backward. But can I have a quarter to buy some bubble gum anyway?"

"Sure you can. Here it is."

And Grandpa went back to reading his newspaper.

UPGRADED PLUS TWO

"Help! Help!" a poor Ten cried as he took to his heels.

"What's the matter? What's happening to you?"

"Don't you see? I'm being chased by a Subtraction. If it catches me, it'll be a disaster."

"Oh, come on! Don't you think 'disaster' is a little much?"

There, the worst has happened: The monstrous Subtraction has grabbed the Ten, lunging at him, slashing savagely with its razor-sharp sword. The poor Ten loses one digit, then another. To its immense good fortune, a foreign car a block long goes by. The Subtraction turns and stares for a moment to see whether he shouldn't shorten it a little, and good old Ten takes advantage of the distraction to get away and hides in a doorway. But now he's no longer a Ten; he's just an ordinary Eight, and what's more, he has a nosebleed.

"Poor little thing, what did they do to you? You got into a fight with your schoolmates, didn't you?"

"Heavens above, everyone run for your lives!" The high-pitched voice is sweet and compassionate, but its owner is Division itself. The unfortunate Eight whispers, "Good evening," in a faint tone, and tries to turn and go, but Division is quicker than the Eight, and with a single clip of her scissors, she cuts him in two: Four and Four. She puts one of the Fours inside her pocket, and the other one takes off running, racing back onto the street, where it leaps onto a passing trolley.

"A moment ago, I was a Ten," he sobs, "and now just look at me! A Four!"

The pupils on the trolley all hasten to get some distance

194

between themselves and the Four. None of them want anything to do with him. The trolley driver mutters, "Certain people really ought to have enough common sense to go on foot."

"But it's not my fault!" the ex-Ten shouts through his tears.

"Sure, blame it on the cat. That's what they all say."

The Four gets off at the next stop, red as a red cherry candy.

Uh oh! He's pulled another one of his pranks—he's stepped on someone's toe.

"I'm sorry! I'm so, so sorry, Signora!"

But the lady isn't angry. In fact, she smiles up at him. Well, well, well, looky who it is! None other than Multiplication!

She has a heart of gold and can't stand the sight of unhappy people. So right then and there, she multiplies the Four by Three. Now, he's a magnificent Twelve, ready to count a whole dozen eggs.

"Hurray!" cries Twelve. "I've been increased! Increased by two."

THE NOTHING MAN

Once upon a time, there was a nothing man. He had a nothing nose, a nothing mouth, he dressed like nothing, and he wore nothing shoes. He went on a trip, heading down a nothing road that went nowhere. He ran into a nothing mouse and asked it, "Aren't you afraid of the cat?"

"No, not at all," replied the nothing mouse. "In this nothing land, there are only nothing cats who have nothing whiskers and nothing claws. What's more, I respect the cheese. I only eat the holes. They taste of nothing, but they're quite sweet."

"My head is spinning," said the little nothing man.

"You have a nothing head. Even if you bang it against the wall, you won't hurt it."

The little nothing man, eager to give it a try, searched high and low for a wall to bang his head against, but it was a nothing wall, and since he'd taken too much of a running start, he came out on the other side. There, too, he found nothing at all—a big, fat nothing.

The little nothing man was so tired of all that nothing that he fell asleep. And while he was sleeping, he dreamed that he was a little nothing man, and he was traveling on a nothing road where he met a nothing mouse, and it, too, ate the holes in the cheese, and the nothing mouse was right: They really did taste like nothing.

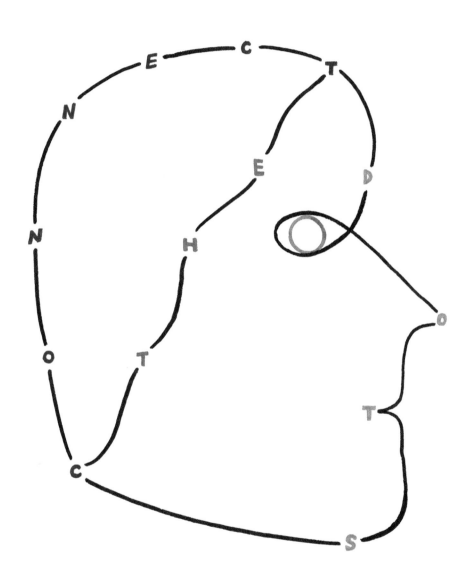

UNIVERSAL HISTORY

In the beginning, the Earth was all wrong, and making it habitable was quite a chore. There were no bridges to get across rivers. There were no trails to climb up mountains. What if you wanted to sit down? Not so much as the shadow of a bench. And if you were dropping from exhaustion? There was no such thing as a bed, nor shoes or boots to keep sharp stones from cutting your feet. If your eyesight was weak, there were no eyeglasses. If you wanted to play a game of soccer, there were no soccer balls. And there was no pasta pot or fire for cooking macaroni. In fact, now that I come to think of it, there wasn't even any pasta. There was nothing at all. Zero plus zero, and that's it. There were only human beings and strong arms with which to work, so the most serious lacks could be corrected. But there are plenty of things still to be righted, so roll up your sleeves! There's plenty of work left to be done!

Table of Contents

www.enchantedlion.com

First US Edition published in 2020 by Enchanted Lion Books,
67 West Street, Studio 403, Brooklyn, NY 11222

Originally published as *Favole al telefono*
Text copyright © 1980, Maria Ferretti Rodari and Paola Rodari, Italy
Text copyright © 1991, Edizioni EL Srl, Trieste Italy
Illustration copyright © 2020 by Valerio
English-language Translation copyright © 2020 by Antony Shuugar
Graphic Design & Layout by Bunker (bnkr.it)

Printed in China
by RR Donnelley Asia Printing Solutions Limited

Second Printing

Library of Congress Cataloging-in-Publication Data

Names: Rodari, Gianni, author. | Vidali, Valerio, 1983- illustrator. |
   Shugaar, Antony, translator.
Title: Telephone tales / Gianni Rodari ; illustrated by Valerio Vidali ;
   translated from Italian by Antony Shugaar.
Other titles: Favole al telefono. English
Description: New York : Enchanted Lion Books, [2019] | Originally published
   in Italian: Turin, Italy : Einaudi, 1962 under the title, Favole al
   telefono. | Hans Christian Anderson Award, 1970. | Summary: A collection
   of nearly seventy short and surreal stories told by Signor Bianchi, a
   traveling salesman, to his daughter over the telephone nightly.
Identifiers: LCCN 2019011908 | ISBN 9781592702848 (hardcover : alk. paper)
Subjects: | CYAC: Storytelling--Fiction. | Humorous stories. | Short stories.
Classification: LCC PZ7.R5987 Te 2019 | DDC [E]--dc23
LC record available at https://lccn.loc.gov/2019011908